UNDERCOVER SCOUT

Jenna Kernan

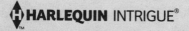

For Jim, always.

ISBN-13: 978-1-335-63916-5

Undercover Scout

Copyright © 2018 by Jeannette H. Monaco

Recycling programs
for this product may
not exist in your area.

This edition published by arrangement with Harlequin Books S.A.

For questions and comments about the quality of this book,
please contact us at CustomerService@Harlequin.com.

® and TM are trademarks of Harlequin Enterprises Limited or its
corporate affiliates. Trademarks indicated with ® are registered in the
United States Patent and Trademark Office, the Canadian Intellectual
Property Office and in other countries.

Printed in U.S.A.

Jenna Kernan has penned over two dozen novels and has received two RITA® Award nominations. Jenna is every bit as adventurous as her heroines. Her hobbies include recreational gold prospecting, scuba diving and gem hunting. Jenna grew up in the Catskills and currently lives in the Hudson Valley in New York State with her husband. Follow Jenna on Twitter, @jennakernan, on Facebook or at jennakernan.com.

Books by Jenna Kernan

Harlequin Intrigue

Apache Protectors: Wolf Den

Surrogate Escape
Tribal Blood
Undercover Scout

Apache Protectors:
Tribal Thunder

Turquoise Guardian
Eagle Warrior
Firewolf
The Warrior's Way

Apache Protectors

Shadow Wolf
Hunter Moon
Tribal Law
Native Born

Harlequin Historical

Gold Rush Groom
The Texas Ranger's Daughter
Wild West Christmas
A Family for the Rancher
Running Wolf

Harlequin Nocturne

Dream Stalker
Ghost Stalker
Soul Whisperer
Beauty's Beast
The Vampire's Wolf
The Shifter's Choice

Visit the Author Profile page at Harlequin.com.

CAST OF CHARACTERS

Dr. Kee Redhorse—The eldest of Colt's brothers and a physician at the tribe's clinic who wants to get Colt psychiatric help. Colt disappears each time he has come looking for him.

Ava Hood—A tribal police detective from a neighboring tribe, she's on the rez to find her missing niece, who is the latest girl to go missing.

Colt Redhorse—Kee's youngest brother, now in protective custody with his wife, Kacey.

Dr. Richard Day—FEMA physician on temporary loan since the dam collapse. He has relatives in the DEA.

Jake Redhorse—Kee's younger brother and a tribal police officer who has been more distant and less forthcoming of late.

Lori Redhorse—Kee's new sister-in-law and a nurse at the tribe's health clinic. She would like to confide in Kee, but Jake has warned her not to interfere with the investigation.

Ty Redhorse—Kee's brother seems to have made a wrong turn for every one of Kee's right choices. Kee hoped that Ty's military service would straighten him out, but he's on the wrong side of the law again.

Jack Bear Den—A Turquoise Guardian and the tribe's only detective.

Wallace Tinnin—Chief of the tribal police force.

Dr. Hector Hauser—The director of the tribe's health clinic and Kee Redhorse's mentor.

Betty Mills—Longtime administrator of the tribe's health clinic.

Louisa Tah—Ava's niece and the most recent girl to go missing.

Yuri Churkin—Russian hired killer on the rez for a contract killing.

Chapter One

Detective Ava Hood watched her prime suspect, Dr. Kee Redhorse, through her field glasses and scowled. You couldn't tell about a person by looking. Dr. Redhorse was a great example of that. Charming, well liked by his tribe, above reproach and the very last person you would suspect. But as it turned out, Ava suspected everyone. And no one was this squeaky clean.

Redhorse was a trusted member of the Turquoise Canyon people. A physician, newly board certified and quite possibly a monster.

She sat in her Chevy Malibu, parked nose out, between the battered yellow bulldozer that created the temporary road and a ten-foot pile of gravel. From her position she could see the FEMA housing trailers that included her sister's and the one assigned to Dr. Richard Day and Dr. Kee Redhorse. She noted in her log that Kee left his assigned FEMA trailer on Sunday to go for a walk at 8:08 a.m., October 15.

Ava didn't trust the tribal police on this rez mostly because Dr. Redhorse had a brother on the force, Jake Redhorse. Plenty of opportunities to look the other way. She knew if she wanted to get to the bottom of her investigation she had to do it herself and she didn't have time for official channels. She accepted the potential risks and didn't care for the cost. State evidence be damned. Justice would be served, one way or another.

Her niece was missing—quite possibly a victim of the series of kidnappings that had recently hit the reservation.

All young women. All to be used as surrogates in a baby trafficking ring run by the Russian mob.

And all of them patients at the clinic shortly before their disappearance. That connection had been made only three weeks ago, ten days before her niece had been taken.

She adjusted her field glasses in her hands and studied her subject. Redhorse was dressed in faded jeans and a college T-shirt, over which he yanked a well-worn, gray hooded sweatshirt as he descended the steps. He looked more approachable in casual clothing, losing some of that air of professionalism that clung to him during his shifts at the tribe's clinic. She tried to ignore the way the clothing hung on his perfect frame and failed.

"No one is that perfect, Ava," she muttered to herself. She knew that much.

Today, he wore scratched and scuffed Timberland boots and a ball cap. He was the sort of man that you noticed right off because of his easy smile and dark, intelligent eyes. Ava noticed him because she thought he was guilty. And if she reacted to him as a man, well, she would ignore it.

How much had he gotten away with in his life because of his good looks and natural appeal? She hated charmers because that was how her grandmother described Ava's father—the father she had never known. *A real charmer.*

She had been watching both doctors from the reservation clinic, Hector Hauser and Kee Redhorse, since last Saturday night. She'd come the minute she'd heard from Sara that one of the missing girls, Kacey Doka, had reappeared after escaping her captors. She'd hoped to speak to Kacey but she and Colt Redhorse had vanished four days ago and she had suspected the Justice Department had them. She'd taken a leave of absence from her own tribe's police force, the Saguaro Flats Apache. She only had a few weeks left in the position. She'd already accepted a new job here on the Turquoise Canyon police force, but the job didn't start until the first of November. That was too long to wait to start her investigation. Time was of the essence and she had to start ASAP. Every good cop knew a missing person's trail got significantly colder after the first forty-eight hours. Her sixteen-year-old niece, Louisa, had been gone for fourteen days and the police here had found nothing.

No, she couldn't trust the Turquoise Canyon tribal force to handle the investigation on their own—especially if one of their officers was blocking evidence.

As far as her force knew, she was here only to comfort her sister, Sara, and help Sara out with her daughters, which was true. But they didn't know she also planned to track down Louisa. That she'd do so alone just made sense. No one else to endanger or to let her down.

Ava had managed to break into both Redhorse's and Hauser's temporary FEMA trailers and install a tracking program on their personal computers. The simple program gave her access to their bank records, email, calendars, browser history and social media accounts. She'd done criminal record checks on each and all their closest associates. The only hit was Kee Redhorse's father, Colton, who was serving a sentence in federal prison for armed robbery. And his brother Ty, who had a juvie record, which was closed. Ava wondered about that one since the dates corresponded exactly to Colton Redhorse's last heist. Even though there had been no other convictions, Ty was currently under investigation by tribal police for kidnapping Kacey Doka—the girlfriend of his youngest brother, Colt. Not enough evidence had been found to tag him to the crime yet, but there was still a big question mark over his head.

And Colt? His record was clean. After Kacey had escaped her captors and fingered Ty as the driver, Ava had confirmed that Kacey and Colt had entered witness protection until the crime ring could be stopped.

"Something that's taking too long in my book," Ava muttered to herself.

Today was day eight of her investigation and she

was running out of time. Soon she'd have to ask for help, return home or resign her job and stay. She thought about resigning from Saguaro Flats force altogether before coming here to Turquoise Canyon, but there were perks to being a cop—even one on leave. She still had access to police databases, which was imperative to her success. Quitting the police force would cause her to lose effectiveness.

She knew the FBI was involved with the investigation because she'd received an alert on her reservation from Turquoise Canyon Tribal Police that they had requested assistance last week after it was discovered that one of their missing persons, Kacey Doka, was not a runaway but a victim of kidnapping who'd identified several other missing girls held captive with her. The Bureau's focus would be on capture and conviction of those responsible. Hers was on recovery by any means.

Ava had already spoken to Kacey's kidnapper. The Russian was paralyzed from the waist down, still in the hospital at Darabee and on suicide watch. Ava got nothing from him as he still elected to pretend he did not speak English. She did get a photo of his tattoos and was running a check on them through the available database. Gang affiliations were often written on the skin and his said Russian organized crime. But they'd need connections here.

First, she'd figure out who and they'd lead her to where the missing were kept. That was the plan. She'd learned all she could from her surveillance of Kee and Hauser and from their personal computers and found nothing to implicate either physician.

She needed to get inside that clinic.

Ava drove along the rutted gravel road, hastily laid before the trailers had been hauled in by the dozens. The dam collapse that touched off the move out of the tribe's tribal seat happened just a little over three weeks ago. The evacuees from lowland areas along the river were moved to temporary shelters out of the potential flood area. The FEMA trailers had arrived and her sister had been among the first to receive one because she had young children.

She parked before her sister's FEMA trailer and ignored the barking as she opened the door. Woody, the big brown family dog, jumped up to say hello. She was surprised to see him, as he had been staying with her sister's mother-in-law, who lived outside the reach of potential flooding. Woody had been added to the family at Louisa's insistence and seeing him made Ava's throat tighten. She gave him a quick scratch behind the ears and pushed him off until he dropped to all fours. His tail swung back and forth, thick and hairless at the base from too much chewing. A shepherd/pit bull mix, he had a head the size and shape of a shovel.

Ava checked her watch. Redhorse should be back by here in about ten minutes. Woody poked around the trailer and returned with a faded, worn, green tennis ball. Ava accepted the offering and tossed the ball. She kept her attention on the end of the street until Redhorse returned.

He was only a few hundred yards away with a newspaper tucked under his arm when he noticed her. She could tell by the hesitation in his stride.

She continued to toss the ball as Redhorse approached.

This was how he found them. Ava throwing a slippery tennis ball to an oversize puppy.

Kee Redhorse's black hair was trimmed short. His skin was tawny-brown with bronze undertones. He had a broad forehead, a blade of a nose that hooked downward over a generous mouth and pinholes in each earlobe for earrings, which he did not wear. Handsome by any standard, she thought.

He hadn't shaved this morning. She found that the dark stubble only added to his appeal. The hair growing beneath his lower lip brought her attention to his mouth. It was a sensual mouth. His lips parted and he inhaled, making his nostrils flare. Then that winning smile appeared. She felt a twitch in her stomach.

Suspect, she reminded herself.

Woody spotted Redhorse and trotted over to say hello. The man offered his hand. It was a nice hand with tight medium brown skin and a sprinkling of dark hair on the back, and the hand itself was broad and square with long elegant fingers. Ava blew away her frustration at her body's reaction to the doctor.

"He's friendly," said Ava and forced a wide

smile as she descended the steps and stood with her hands in her back pockets. She'd dressed for success today, in jeans that left room for her ankle holster but hugged everything else and a blouse that was feminine without broadcasting her cup size. Woody sniffed Redhorse's hand and the wet ball fell to the ground.

Ava made a grab for the ball but Woody was too quick and snatched it up again. The tug-of-war ensued with the dog crouched, growling as he shook his shovel of a head, tail thumping. Ava wasn't much of a frolicker but she did her best.

Redhorse laughed. "He's not giving up."

"He loves to play," she said.

Woody won. The canine dropped the ball at Redhorse's feet.

Traitor, she thought.

"He wants you to throw it," she said keeping her smile until he turned to retrieve the ball.

He did and it was a really good throw. She gauged his physical strength and was glad she had both her service weapon and her training.

Woody returned, chewing as he trotted. He folded to the ground to begin gnawing in earnest, the ball between his paws. She could swear the canine was smiling.

Ava put a hand on her hip and sighed.

"Guess I finally wore him out," she said and gave Redhorse another smile, making eye contact. He seemed to be looking right through her. Heat sizzled inside her and her stomach tensed. She knew he was single, dated occasionally but never for long and had been engaged to an Anglo in med school. Circumstances of the breakup were unclear.

Redhorse cleared his throat and looked back to the dog. Ava took a deep breath and pinched her lips together as she fought the troubling physical zip of awareness for him. It had never happened to her with a suspect before.

He cast her an effortless smile and the tug grew stronger. She was going to have to arrest him or sleep with him.

Yeah, right. She didn't have the justification for either action.

Their eyes met and her heart gave an irritating flutter again. She wished she had enough evidence to read him his rights. She bet handcuffs would wipe that smile off his face.

Her grandmother would approve, she thought. Also possibly a felon. She scowled.

Redhorse was a suspect, not a prospect.

Woody stared up at her, his ball forgotten.

She pointed. "That's Woody."

Her gaze dropped to the sensual curve of his upper lip.

You're staring at his mouth.

He switched to Tonto Apache. "Hello. I am Roadrunner born of Wolf, the oldest son of Colton and May Redhorse." Then he switched back to English as he completed his introduction and extended his free hand. "I'm Doctor Kee Redhorse."

Trotting out the title, she thought. She didn't trust him and did not accept his hand. She was already attracted to the man. Touching him would only make the nagging stab of desire worse. Instead, Ava lifted her hands out before her, palms up.

"Wet," she said, with dog slobber.

He held his smile as his arm dropped to his side. Was he disappointed?

"I live just up that way," he said, motioning the way he had come. "For now anyway. Until we move back to Piñon Flats."

She knew that. Likely knew more about him than his own family.

Since the dam collapsed upriver of this reservation, most of the residents of the community of Piñon Flats had been relocated here to high ground in Turquoise Canyon while the temporary rubble dam was reinforced by FEMA. Their permanent houses were still intact, but the dam had already been destroyed in an act of eco-extremism. Neither the tribe elders nor FEMA wanted to put anyone else at risk.

"I heard that will be any day," she said.

He nodded and grinned.

"How is it I have never seen you before?" he asked and switched to Tonto. "I know that I would remember you."

That smile made her insides roll and her stomach flutter. It was like swimming against a strong current. Those teeth, that jawline, that elegant nose. Oh, boy, was she in over her head. She hoped he wasn't guilty because…what? He was handsome? She was smitten? She needed to get a grip.

It wasn't her job to hope he was guilty or innocent. It was her job to find Louisa. If he had her or was responsible for her disappearance, then that was that.

Ava, you need to lock this down.

"I didn't get your name," said Kee.

"I'm Ava Hood." She didn't use her legal name, her father's name. Never had, though her surname, Yokota, did crop up on things like her diplomas and legal documents.

"You didn't grow up on the rez, Ava. I'd have noticed you." His smile was so dazzling she needed sunglasses. Suddenly his charm and charisma seemed a threat. It made it easier to resist.

"I am Snake born of Spider," she said in perfect Tonto Apache in the traditional form of greeting. One always began with the tribe, moved to clans and then relations. Only after these important ties were given, did one mention their own name. "My parents are Eldon and Lydia Hood from Saguaro Flats reservation." Though her father was Eldon Yokota, she had given the correct first name.

"You speak very well," he said in English.

The compliment seemed an insult. Besides, she had little choice as her grandmother had no other language but Tonto and she had lived with her until she was eight.

"I know that rez. Small, right?"

"Very."

"What brings you up here?"

"Visiting my sister. She married a man up here."

"What's his name?"

"Diamond Tah."

Kee's smile slipped. "Oh." He nodded and then met her gaze, his smile gone and his eyes serious. "I knew him very well. I used to listen to him play the flute at gatherings. So your sister is—"

"Sara Tah."

Ava's sister was newly widowed. Her husband had died one night on his way to the bathroom from a brain aneurysm. He'd been forty-two. That should have been enough tragedy for one year, but it turned out to be only the start.

His gaze flicked away again. Was that guilt? Or did he know that her sister was in far worse shape since her husband's death than Ava had imagined. The drinking had gotten worse and there had been calls to protective services. It was reason enough for Ava to visit.

Ava waited for him to speak. What would a man who she suspected had a hand in the kidnappings say at this moment?

"I'm very sorry," he said.

Appropriate, she thought.

"For what?"

He looked surprised, as if this was obvious, but she wanted to hear him say it. "Sara lost her husband recently and now…well, Louisa is missing. I know she's been…struggling. It's a terrible tragedy."

He did not do or say anything that might reveal that he could be the reason for Louisa's disappearance.

"We are still hopeful."

"Of course." He shifted uncomfortably. "How is Sara doing?"

Did he know about her sister's drinking?

She went on the defensive. It was her fallback position, and protecting her sister came naturally as breathing. The truth was that her sister had lost weight, and didn't eat. The entire situation made Ava's chest hurt. "It's a hard time."

He nodded. "And the girls?"

She wanted to press a finger into his broad chest and tell him that he didn't have the right to ask about them. Not ever.

"They're frightened, mostly. The twins are afraid to leave for school or take the bus. So I'm driving them, for now."

Margarita and Alexandra were five, and Olivia, only three. These were the children Sara had with Diamond. She'd brought Louisa to the marriage after her first marriage had failed.

Redhorse had treated each one of her sister's kids. Most damning, he'd treated Louisa on September

30, on her last visit to the tribe's clinic, just two days before her disappearance.

"I understand that," he said. "Good of you to be with her at this time. Are you her younger sister?"

"Why do you ask?"

He cast her a shy smile. "You look young."

"I am the younger sister but not by much. I'm twenty-eight."

He looked shocked. She got that a lot but not looking her age had advantages. People often underestimated her.

She watched him. He didn't shift or rub his neck. His gaze did not cut away as if he were anxious to put her behind him. He only held the appropriate look of sadness and concern.

He smiled. "Nice folks."

"They sure are. I'd do anything for my sister and her kids." She waited through the awkward pause. Still, he radiated nothing but concern.

"Is that why you bumped into me? You wanted to ask me about them?"

He was smart. She'd give him that but that only made him more dangerous if he was guilty.

"Is there something you'd like to get off your chest?" she asked.

"Off my...me? No," he said and looked puzzled.

She waited as he cocked his head to study her, brow wrinkling.

"Well, it's a pleasure to meet you, Ava. May I call you Ava?"

She nodded.

"And please call me Kee."

She preferred to call him prime suspect.

"What do you do down there on your rez, Ava?"

"Why do you ask?"

"I'm not sure. You have a certain directness to you."

The pause seemed especially long. He stared at her and she noted the golden flecks in his deep brown eyes.

"So what do you do down there on the flats?" he asked again.

"I used to work for the casino. Dealer. High rollers, mostly. But I'm taking a break." Actually that was her sister's bio but she wasn't going to tell him she was ROTC, had done four years of active duty in Germany and had just finished her four additional years on reserve while completing police training, and recently earned her gold shield. Given how her sister had completely withdrawn from society after her husband's death and buried herself in a bottle, she doubted that Sara would have the opportunity to blow her cover.

The small talk continued. He told her what she already knew, that their clinic had only seven employees. Two physicians. One administrator, Betty Mills, and five nurses, one of whom—Lori Mott Redhorse—was well on her way to becoming a midwife. Lori was also Kee's sister-in-law and the one who'd first made the connection between the clinic and the six missing women from his tribe.

Ava had already spoken with Lori and believed she was one of the good guys. The woman seemed interested in finding the missing teenagers and willing to do all she could to help the investigation. Not the actions of someone guilty of a crime.

"I thought there were three physicians," Ava said when she caught an inaccuracy in Redhorse's story.

"Oh, yes. That's right. Dr. Day is on loan from FEMA. That's my roommate, temporarily, until we get the all-clear to move back home." Since Ava had searched the trailer, she was aware of the roommate situation. But Dr. Day hadn't been around long enough to be a suspect, so she'd focused entirely on Dr. Kee Redhorse.

"I didn't know that FEMA provided doctors."

"Oh, yeah. And they have emergency medical response teams. Our clinic is currently set up in two of their mobile medical units. Crowded, but we are getting the job done. It's been good to have another set of hands during the crisis. We've been super busy but we'll lose Day soon."

She quirked a brow. "That so?"

He casually slipped a hand into his back pocket. She watched his hands, wondering if he had a weapon. Kee kept talking.

"Once we get back to the clinic in Piñon Flats and out of those trailers, I'm sure they'll recall him. Too bad, he's a nice guy."

There was something implied in his tone. She took a guess. "But not a good doctor?"

The side of his mouth quirked. His tell, she decided, that little gesture that said she had made the right guess. "He's adequate."

"But not Native."

Kee made a sound that might have been a laugh. "Oh, I don't mind that. But he is from Minnesota. So he thinks it's too hot up here."

"He'd hate Saguaro Flats."

Now Kee did laugh. The sound buzzed over her skin and the hairs on her neck lifted at the pure musical joy in that deep male rumble of delight. She was reconsidering her strategy. Ava had not anticipated liking her suspect.

"His specialty is emergency medicine. He's less interested in ongoing treatment of chronic conditions and I think he's had his fill of diabetes and high blood pressure."

"I see."

Woody discovered an abandoned soda bottle, which he trotted over to Ava with. Her attempts to retrieve it from his mouth resulted in another game of chase.

"He can have it," said Ava, recognizing defeat first. She turned back to her questioning. "How do you like working at the clinic?"

He shifted his weight from one leg to the other. "Oh, I like it, but I really prefer emergency medicine, too. Plus I'm only here part-time. Just finishing up my residency. Dr. Hauser, he's our head physician, he arranged for me to split my time between here and Darabee Hospital."

Ava crinkled up her face. "Sounds busy."

Kee shrugged, a good-natured expression on his face. "It is. Doesn't leave much time for a social life—or even a chance to catch up with the people in my own family. And since the dam collapse the clinic hours have been crazy. But I love the work and with my loans…" He held a hand to his throat and pretended to be strangling. "Gotta get a position in a hospital. Plan is to leave for a few years to get the best salary possible. I hope to come back someday."

That didn't mesh with a man making oodles of money from the Russian mob unless he knew that his tribal police force had made connections between the missing girls and his clinic. Then crying poverty was smart. His little brother was on the force. Had Officer Jake Redhorse given Kee some insider info?

"Medical school is expensive," she said, hoping she sounded sympathetic. Her computer-hacking had exposed he was in up to his eyeballs in debt and had a really good motive for wanting to make a boatload of fast cash.

"I've had some assistance from the tribe. Dr. Hauser helped me qualify for a grant that covered some of it."

She made a mental note to check on that.

"Sounds like a great guy." *Or a dangerous criminal*, she thought.

"Yeah. He is. Hector is the one who encouraged me to practice medicine. I had a leg-length discrepancy as a kid." He shrugged. "He took an interest."

She thought of the photo she'd seen in his room in the FEMA trailer. He'd been younger, with a single crutch under one thin arm.

"I had lots of surgeries down in Phoenix." He held his arms wide. "Now I'm the shortest male in my family."

He wasn't short, by any means. She marked him at nearly six feet.

"Why is that?" she asked.

"Well, they can't add to the shorter leg. You know, make you taller. So they make corrections by reducing the size of the longer limb."

She flinched as she imagined someone sawing through her lower leg bone.

"Yeah, exactly. Lost three inches. But they even up within an eighth of an inch." He bent slightly at the waist and presented his straight legs for her examination. They were fine muscular legs. She could see that even through the denim of his jeans. "Hector arranged for all that and the therapy. Pulled strings and it was all taken care of."

So Hector was a string puller and Kee was forever in his debt. How far would Kee go to pay him back?

"It was a hard time. My dad was...gone."

In prison, she thought.

"We didn't have much money."

"Your head physician sounds like a wonderful man." Her smile felt tight and unnatural. Kee didn't seem to notice.

"He used to operate out of a room at tribal headquarters when I was a kid. Gave me all my shots there. But you should see the facility now. We have an urgent care center, triage, three exam rooms, reception, radiology and a woman's health center with three birthing rooms, plus additional ob-gyn exam rooms."

"That's impressive. Paid through gaming?" she asked. It wasn't, she knew, because she'd seen their budget, via her sister's login on the tribe's website. Some areas of the tribe's website were public while others were password-protected to ensure only tribal members could access them. The page holding the minutes from tribal government meetings was one of these pages.

Kee shrugged. "Our administrator handles all that."

Betty Mills, Ava knew. Recently divorced. Mother of three grown boys and driving an Audi leased by the clinic.

Woody tore the bottle in two and Ava threw the ball so she could retrieve the jagged pieces.

"I better check on my sister and the girls." Sara was probably still in bed and likely hungover. The girls were being raised by a game console, as far as

Ava could tell. She could at least get them all out of bed and feed them a healthy breakfast.

Anything to keep them all afloat until Louisa and the other missing children could be found.

"Oh," he looked disappointed. "Of course. Umm, Ava? Will you be here a few days?"

"I plan to be. Yes."

"Would you like to have a drink sometime this week?" His face was red when he finished, which she was chagrined to find she found absolutely adorable. Her heart was not behaving, hammered as if this was something other than a stakeout. Her department had another word for it...*entrapment*.

She didn't care. All rules were off when you messed with hers.

So, here it was, the opportunity she had been hoping for. But that was before she realized she would be attracted to the good doctor. She hesitated, biting her bottom lip as she tapped the two sides of the ruined plastic bottle together before her in a nervous tattoo.

Dating Kee would give her access to him, to Hauser and to the clinic and she needed to know what was going on in there.

"Ava?" His dark brow lifted. "Are you seeing someone?"

She shook her head. "Oh, no. Not currently." It was unfortunate that not one of the men in her past made her silly heart pitter-patter like this one, here.

"I just need to work around the kids' schedules and my sister. And I don't really drink."

Because it meant a possible loss of control and Ava did not go there.

"Oh. Coincidence," he said. "Neither do I. And I understand about your family. You're here for them. Family first, my dad always said."

How reassuring. An adage from a con.

As far as she could tell Kee and Jake were the only ones that visited dear old dad and not often. But at least they had a dad.

"My sister gets home from work at five fifteen. I've been getting the kids dinner and I'm free after that."

"Oh, great."

"When?" she asked.

"How about Tuesday? Dinner at the casino?"

Ava was known here as Sara's sister and a member of the Saguaro Flats tribe. But like many detectives, she kept her profession secret mainly so as not to make people uncomfortable but also to allow her to more easily do her job. Anyone who would have asked was told that she worked in her tribe's adult education program, her usual cover.

"That sounds fun." Ava held her smile.

"I'll pick you up around six?"

"Seven."

"Sure," Kee agreed.

She drew a pen from her back pocket. "Give me your hand."

He did. His palm slid across hers, warm and dry. The tingle of awareness began at her fingers and rippled up her arm. Whatever attraction was between them was as strong as it was unwanted. She stared up at him, meeting his welcoming brown eyes. Then she used her teeth to remove the cap to the pen and she wrote her cell phone number on the back of his hand. Her task done, she was both anxious and reluctant to let him go. She did and stepped back, sitting on the step of her sister's trailer.

"Now, don't scrub up before you copy that," she teased lightly.

He studied the back of his hand and grinned. "I won't."

His smile made her insides tumble as if she were spinning. She had no trouble returning his grin and that worried her.

"See you Tuesday, Dr. Redhorse."

"Kee, please."

"I'll try to remember that."

Ava smiled against the chill that swept through her. If he was behind this, she'd see he never got within sight of another girl for as long as he lived.

Chapter Two

Monday afternoon the tribe's urgent care center had gone from crazy to ridiculous. Since the dam collapse in September there was no more normal. Kee had hoped that with the arrival of FEMA things would get better. But the EMTs had just brought him another patient. He knew this one. Not unusual on such a small reservation. But this one was the son of his high school friend Robert Corrales.

Robert had the boy when they were in tenth grade and Robbie Junior was now twelve years old. But he wouldn't make thirteen if Kee didn't stop the bleeding.

Lori Mott assisted and he was happy for the extra hands. *Redhorse*, his mind corrected. She was no longer a Mott, since she had married his younger brother Jake, less than a month ago. Kee kept forgetting to call her Lori Redhorse. His brother had married the nurse so fast, he still hadn't gotten accustomed to the change.

Kee assessed the damage. The EMTs had done a fair job stopping the bleeding on his arm. But his head wound wasn't the same story. The plate-glass window had opened a gash on Robbie's forehead that was giving Kee trouble. Lori kept pressure on that wound, allowing him the time he needed to clamp the artery Robbie had sliced open in his right forearm. Either one was hemorrhaging fast enough to kill him. The boy was pale from shock and blood loss, his lips had gone blue and his skin had taken on the ghastly pallor of a corpse.

"Got it," he said. "I'll finish that after I stitch his head."

"The EMT said he didn't think he could make it to Darabee," said Lori.

"He was right." Kee quickly stitched the gash that ran in a jagged line from the boy's hairline to above the outer edge of his eyebrow.

Lori shook her head as she assessed the lacerations. "I'll get another Ringer's lactate. You want plasma?"

"No. This should do."

Lori left him to use the computer terminal at the intake station in the FEMA trailer that now served as their urgent care facility. When she came back with the fluids he had the gash closed.

"As soon as he's stable, arrange transport to Darabee," said Kee.

Darabee was only twenty miles away but with the river road under construction and the switchbacks leading down the mountain the ride was thirty to forty minutes from Piñon Forks, and from Turquoise Ridge, where the clinic had been temporarily placed, it was more like an hour.

Lori finished inserting the IV and nodded. "You got it. His dad is waiting."

"He needs a vascular surgeon if he's going to keep that hand."

"Betty is calling over. They'll have one." She smiled at him. His sister-in-law, he realized. Jake was a lucky man. He was so happy the two had finally worked out their differences.

"Good work, Kee."

Kee stripped off his gloves as Dr. Hector Hauser stepped into the curtained examining area.

"Need a hand?" he asked.

"We got it," said Kee.

Lori pulled the blood pressure cuff off the wall and slipped it around Robbie's thin arm.

Hauser looked around at the amount of blood and bloody gauze and gave a low whistle. He checked the boy's pupils and his pulse.

"Weak," he said and then checked the IV bag suspended on the stainless-steel rack.

Day poked his head into the room. "Need a hand?"

Before he could answer, Hauser waved him off. "We got it."

Kee gave Day an apologetic shrug. Day's mouth was a grim line as he sighed and returned the way he had come.

"I'll speak to the dad," said Hauser.

"You know his expertise is emergency medicine. Right?" Kee lifted his chin toward the exam area Day occupied. "He's taken the FEMA emergency medical specialist training. And he's board certified."

"Well, if the trailer collapses, I'll be sure to call him."

Hauser returned a few minutes later with Robbie's younger brother, Teddy, who had a gash on his lower leg.

"Parents didn't even see this one," said Hector. "Cut himself getting to his brother." He switched to Tonto. "You are a hero, son. Got his big brother help in time."

Teddy gave him a confused stare. Hector's smile dropped. "Did you understand that?"

Teddy shook his head.

Hector sighed. It was a crusade of his, that children learn their language. He held Teddy's hand and steered the boy out of the curtained area and right into the boys' parents.

Robert Corrales turned to Kee but peered past him to his older boy. "Is Robbie going to be okay?"

"He'll need some surgery at Darabee. But, yes, he's going to make it."

Robert threw himself at Kee, forcing Kee to take a step back as Robert hugged him. His wife joined in and Kee was pressed like chicken salad between two slices of bread. Weeping and *thank-you*s blurred together. Lori took Teddy into the exam area beside Robbie's to wait for Dr. Hauser, and the parents crossed through the curtain to their oldest child.

It was another twenty minutes more before Kee

was satisfied that Robbie was ready for transport. Robert accompanied his son and his wife remained with Teddy.

Once his patient was off, Kee waited for Hector to finish stitching up Teddy's lower leg. Kee was aiming for the momentary pause between one patient and the next to speak to Hector about his decision to resign from the clinic. Kee had agonized about leaving at such a time, but his mother had decided to foster the three teenage Doka girls. A wonderful act on her part, but unfortunately, a decision that would leave Kee without a place to live once they returned to Piñon Flats. The young fosterlings would need the space. Kee had moved in with his mother to help decrease his monthly expenses, and it was unrealistic of him to expect to afford a place of his own on his current salary. Not with the massive medical school debt hanging over his head.

Dr. Hauser had been only slightly older than he was now when Kee had first met him in the tribe's health clinic. He had not known at the time that meeting Hector would change his life. Kee wanted nothing more than to stay on his reservation and tend the sick and injured on Turquoise Canyon. But you did not always get what you wanted. And he had financial obligations that could no longer be put off.

Hector glanced up at Kee over the thick black rims of his transition lenses. His hairline had receded to the point where he had more forehead than hair. What was left was trimmed short so you could see the single gold medicine shield earring he wore in his right earlobe. Kee frowned as he noticed the diagonal earlobe crease, knowing that it was a possible indicator of coronary artery disease.

Hauser lifted his brow, making his forehead a field of furrows. "What's up?" he asked.

"I need a minute."

"Sure. Hand me that gauze." He pointed with a thick finger, his light russet skin a sharp contrast against the white of his lab coat. The dam collapse, which had necessitated them moving into the temporary FEMA trailers, had tripled their workload. Kee had never expected any sort of terrorism to touch his little corner of Arizona. But he thought that the extra load might be too much for Hector, judging from the puffy circles beneath his eyes.

Kee handed over the gauze and Dr. Hauser stripped off the outer covering, then expertly wrapped the boy's leg in a herringbone pattern that would prevent slipping.

"There, now," he said to the boy. "All done."

The boy still had tear tracks on his cheeks but he was quiet now that the Novocain was working and the blood had been mopped up. Hauser turned to the boy's mother. "Give him some Tylenol when you get him home. Two 80 mg tablets, three times a day, for today only, and keep this dry. Bring him back in ten days and I'll take out the stitches."

The boy swung his legs off the table and glanced at Hauser.

"Go on. You can walk on it. But no running or swimming or scratching!" He held out his hand to shake. Teddy hesitated but took Hector's hand. "Good work today, Teddy. You should be proud. You take care of your brother and look after your mom."

Teddy nodded his acceptance of this duty and slid to the floor. It was what Kee's dad had said to him before the sentencing. Ironic, since his father had never done so. He was a living example of what happened when you made your own rules.

The pair headed out of the curtained exam room. Hauser followed to the hall.

"Give me a minute, Lori," he called.

Lori Redhorse waved in acknowledgment, taking charge of the boy and his mother, ushering them out.

Dr. Day popped his head out of the exam area beside Hauser's.

"Mrs. Cruz says she wants to see you," he said to Hauser.

"Well, of course she does. She's been seeing me since she was born." He muttered something, and Kee caught the word *worthless*. "In a minute." Hauser glanced at Kee, motioning with his head. Kee followed. They paused halfway between Day's examining area and the reception table, where Lori sat at the computer.

Hauser's mouth turned down, making him look like one of the largemouth bass Kee loved to catch. Hauser shook his head. "That ambulance arrived.

He—" Hauser jerked his head toward Dr. Day's examining area "—didn't even step out to check on it. He must have heard it. You sure did."

Kee shrugged, having no explanation.

"I swear he needs more looking after than the babies in our NICU. What kind of doctors do they have at FEMA anyway?" He tugged at the black stethoscope looped around his thick neck.

"Give him a chance."

"Nobody wants to see him. Besides, this is my clinic. Up until now that is. The tribal council has no right to meddle here."

The dam collapse gave them every right, Kee thought, but said nothing.

Requests like Mrs. Cruz's had been happening a lot lately but Kee could not figure why so many patients were being so difficult. The clinic was short-staffed and the tribe had managed to get FEMA to provide them with an extra hand. Richard Day seemed nice enough, but he sure was not a hit with patients.

"So…" said Hauser, changing the subject. "How was the interview?"

Kee was a finalist for a position at St. Martin's Medical Center in Phoenix. It was internal medicine and he preferred emergency medicine and he also preferred to live here with his tribe instead of out there. But beggars could not be choosers. He'd been shocked at how fast the loans came due once he finished the last of his educational requirements.

Now he stared up from a seemingly bottomless pit of debt. It would take years and years to get clear of them and return to the tribe. Reaching his dreams had come at a high cost. The ironic part was that his ambition was to help his tribe members the way Hauser had once helped him. Now, instead, he'd be miles away treating strangers.

"They've offered me a position," said Kee.

"Not surprised. But I hope you'll consider ours, as well."

Kee's brows lifted. He hadn't known that was a possibility and had assumed there would be no place for him. With his residency completed, he needed a job.

"What about Dr. Day?"

"He's temporary. Once we get back to the clinic at Piñon Flats, we'll be able to handle the load with two doctors. Maybe add a physician's assistant."

They'd had this discussion before. When he got his residency in Darabee, just off the rez, Hauser had managed to keep Kee here part-time and count the hours toward his residency requirements.

"My mother is fostering the Doka girls," said Kee.

"I heard that. She brought them in for a checkup. Malnourished and need some dental work, but nothing your mom can't handle."

"The point is, eventually I'll need a place to live." Sharing a FEMA trailer with Dr. Day worked for now, giving him easy access to the temporary clinic.

But they expected to be back in their permanent facility this week.

"I see. The Doka girls have taken your bedroom, I imagine."

Kee nodded. "Dr. Hauser, I need to start repayment on my loans. I can't afford to work here part-time." *And I don't know how much longer I can survive with only work, work and more work, with only a few hours of sleep in between.*

He'd been living with his mom, but he'd had so little time to spend with her, he barely knew how the transition with the Doka girls was going. And he hadn't seen his brothers Colt or Ty since a week ago Saturday when they'd driven off on Ty's motorcycle after he and Jake had tried and failed to get Colt to seek help for his PTSD. Jake had told him that Colt had been seen and released. Kee worried about Colt living up in the woods at the family's mining claim since he'd come home from Afghanistan. Jake said Colt took off every time he went up there. Only Ty had succeeded in reaching him.

"Listen, is this about your living situation or your loans?"

"Both."

"Easy. My grant to hire you was approved."

Kee fiddled with the head of his stethoscope. "I need a permanent posting."

"Five years sound permanent enough?"

Kee didn't keep the surprise from his voice. "Five?"

"Yes, includes housing. In the new housing in Piñon Flats. We're building especially for the tribal employees. Doctors get priority. Should take about three months, so you can move in by Christmas. We'll all be in the same area near the clinic. Three bedrooms, garage and screened deck. You get an auto allowance of $500 a month. Plus forgiveness of your loans for working in a rural facility if you stay the full five years."

"And the salary?"

After Dr. Hauser's response, Kee's hands dropped to his sides. He blinked in shock.

"Plus a five percent cost of living raise each year," Hauser added.

Kee had been embarrassed to accept the Big Money his brother Ty had offered. Big Money was the sum total of each tribe member's royalties from the casino held in trust and released when each member reached their majority. Ty's money amounted to eighteen thousand and had kept Kee's head just above water, covering his living expenses during medical school in Phoenix. Without it, Kee could not have completed his education. With the salary Hauser had just offered, he could pay his brother back and fix his mother's car.

Hauser was still talking. "So about the auto stipend—get rid of that wreck you drive."

The 2004 midnight blue RAM pickup truck had been used when he bought it. The only reason it was still running was because Ty fixed it for free.

"Besides," Hauser continued. "I'm used to you. I don't like breaking in new physicians." He thumbed toward the corridor and Dr. Day.

"Why didn't you tell me this before today?" Kee had been interviewing from Flagstaff to Tucson and was heartsick at having to leave the rez, especially now. People were moving and building and naturally getting hurt in the process. Accidents due to drinking were way up and there was a troubling spike in heroin overdoses.

"I only got word today. Email's in my computer. It's just been approved by our oversight board. So, you need time to think about it?"

"Forgiveness of all my loans? I have five."

"All."

"Private and government?"

"All means all," said Hauser.

Kee felt the weight of his burden lifting off his shoulders and he almost felt like dancing. He laughed.

"Well, then yes." Kee grinned. "I could work with that."

Hauser extended his hand and they shook. His mentor reeled him in and wrapped an arm around Kee's shoulders.

"Good, good. I've been thinking. I've been here doing this thirty-five years. When the time comes to turn over the reins, I'd like that someone to be you."

Kee was speechless.

Hauser let him go and spoke in Tonto. "You are like a second son to me."

Kee felt the hitch in his throat and didn't think he could speak.

"You know Turquoise Canyon," said Hauser. "You are a part of this place. You belong here with your people." He switched back to English. "Besides, I'll be damned if I'll lose you to some big city hospital when you are needed right here."

"I'm honored to follow your example, sir."

"Well, it's settled, then. I'll get you the paperwork. Get it back when you can."

Kee felt humbled. This man was all he ever wanted to become and earning his respect…well, Kee was brimming with joy. All the hard work and effort was paying off. Hauser had called him a second son. Kee thought he might cry.

"Now we have to find you a nice girl, hmm?"

Kee flushed. That was an odd thing to say. "Time still for that."

"No time like the present. Pay off the loans. Find a wife and have a few children. You'll be all set. Settled. A man the community can trust."

That was a strange way of saying it, thought Kee. He thought he'd build trust by having a sterling reputation and all the necessary credentials. Unlike his father and Ty, Kee had steered clear of trouble and taken the road that involved hard work and sacrifice.

"My wife has a niece you should meet. She's

beautiful, traditional and lives in Koun'nde," he said naming one of their three settlements.

"Well, we'll see."

Hauser clapped him on the shoulder. "Good man." Then he turned to go, waving a hand in farewell. "Patients waiting."

The female voice came from behind them. "Dr. Hauser?"

Kee knew that voice. It was the clinic administrator, Betty Mills.

Hauser turned and smiled at the woman who kept the place running. Betty was in her middle years, with onyx eyes and hair to match. She dressed better than anyone Kee knew, with never a hair out of place. Her makeup was thick and meticulous from the liner to the bright unnatural pink of her lips. High heels and the jangling gold bracelets she always wore on her left arm announced her on each approach. Betty loved her bling. Even the chain that held her reading glasses on the bright purple blouse was gold with clear crystal beads.

"There's my boss," said Hauser to Kee and winked. "What's up, Betty?"

"Waiting room is full and so we've set up lawn chairs outside. They're full now, too. You both need to pick up the pace." She snapped her fingers, the long acrylic nails painted purple to match her outfit.

Hauser winked at Kee and then scuttled down the corridor to the exam area where Dr. Day waited.

Betty gave Kee a critical stare. "I'll tell Lori you're ready for the next one."

Down the corridor, Dr. Day stepped out of the examination area rubbing his neck. Hauser frowned after him and then drew the curtains closed behind him.

Hauser had not liked Day since the minute the tribal council had informed him that they had voted to get them extra help. It seemed Hector did not mind being bossed by Betty, but he did not like the tribal council interfering with *his* clinic.

Dr. Day reached Kee and gave him a defeated look. "All I did was ask if he'd speak in English when I'm there."

"I can imagine how that went over," said Kee, feeling sympathy for the doctor who was struggling to fit in with the local culture.

Kee glanced to the receiving station and the young mother carrying a crying toddler in his direction. He smiled and motioned them into the free exam area.

She spoke to him in Tonto Apache and Kee answered in kind. He could not believe how lucky he was to be able to stay here in the place he loved with the people he knew. A house. A car and a salary that was more money than he could even imagine. It seemed nearly too good to be true.

Chapter Three

Tuesday morning at the temporary clinic was crazy, made more so by the fact that Dr. Day did not appear at his usual time. Kee covered the women's health clinic, now in the adjoining trailer, and Hauser took the urgent care center. Kee called Day several times but got no answer.

Hauser popped into Kee's exam area.

"Anything?" he asked.

"No answer on his phone."

"FEMA sent us a dud."

Kee didn't think Hauser was giving Day a chance. He almost seemed to be undercutting his efforts. Kee didn't understand it because he'd never seen Hauser act like this.

Hauser waved a dismissive hand. "Social skills of a tortoise and just as much personality."

Kee was now officially really worried. He knew Day had set out with his Subaru at seven, his mountain bike strapped onto the vehicle's bike rack, and that he was always back by just after eight thirty, which was why he was usually late for their 9 a.m. opening. Still, he was never *this* late. Something felt off but he told himself to be patient.

Kee glanced at his watch. Day had been missing for hours.

When they reached noon and Kee still had no word, he called his brother Jake Redhorse.

"When did you see him last?" asked Jake.

"This morning. He was going for a ride before work."

"On a horse?" asked Jake.

"He rides his bike. Mountain biking."

"Okay, yup. I've seen him. Looks like a giant canary escaping a coal mine?"

Kee thought of the bright yellow exercise gear Dr. Day wore when biking and smiled.

"Yeah, that's him."

"I'll put the word out, but I'm down at the worksite on the river. I'll call FEMA. Meanwhile, you got a neighbor who could see if his car is there? Maybe check the house?"

Kee thought of Ava Hood. She lived just down the street.

"Yeah. I have someone."

Kee gave Jake the details on Day's vehicle.

"Let me know if the neighbor finds him."

"Will do."

Kee disconnected and held the phone to his chest a moment. He was going to call Ava. He hoped that she was at her sister's trailer, right down the road from his. He had already put Ava's number in his contacts. He blew out a breath and made the call.

He explained the situation. "Could you check if his car is in the drive?"

"Hold on. I'm walking out the door now."

He heard a door open and close.

"He ever do this before?" she asked.

"He bikes every morning. And he's late every morning. But not like this."

"Does he have someone here, somewhere he might be?"

"He might have a girlfriend down on the flats somewhere and a brother in some kind of law enforcement. DEA or ICE? I can't remember. Alphabet soup, you know? But I saw him this morning and it's a work day."

"Almost there," said Ava. "Yeah. Okay. No Subaru. No other vehicle. You want me to look inside?"

"Door is locked."

"I'm looking in the front door window now. Big hook on the wall in the entrance."

"For his bike," said Kee.

"It's empty. I'm knocking." He heard the pounding knock and the silence that followed. "No one here, Kee."

Kee pressed his free hand to his forehead. "So he's still out there."

"Call Chief Tinnin. Report him missing. Do you know the route he takes?"

Kee squeezed his eyes shut thinking. "He has several."

"What are they?"

He relayed the routes he knew and she said she'd drive them. Kee called Jake again. His brother assured him he'd report that Day was unaccounted for. Kee went back to work with a cold knot in his stomach. He just felt something was wrong.

He was just finishing a round of immunizations on an eighteen-month-old when the phone rang. He snatched it out of his pocket right there in the exam room. It was Ava. A glance at the clock showed that it was three in the afternoon. Kee punched the receive button and lifted the phone to his ear.

"I found Day's car," Ava said.

He pressed his hand to his forehead. "Where?"

She told him.

"That's the trailhead to the ruins," said Kee.

"Hard to know which way he went from there," she said. "Lots of trails through the cliff dwellings. Right?"

"My brother Ty has a dog. She's an excellent tracker."

There was a long pause.

"Ava?"

"Yeah, call him. Meet me here."

"Should I call the police?" he asked.

"Up to you. Would Ty want the police here?" she asked matter-of-factly.

He pressed his lips together. Ava was just a visitor on their rez and yet she knew about Ty. She likely knew about their father, as well. "I'll wait."

"We need something of Day's," said Ava. "Something he recently wore or frequently wears, to help the dog find his scent."

Kee swallowed at this and then raked a hand through his black hair. "I'll stop at the trailer and find something. Meet you there at the trailhead in ten."

AVA LEANED AGAINST her Malibu in the bright golden light of the crisp late afternoon. The blue sky and bird sounds belied her mood. Day had parked in a parking area before the lower ruins. His pale blue Subaru was covered with a fine coating of red dust, so it had been here awhile. It did not make sense that he'd be here all day when he was supposed to be at work.

She checked her service weapon and then returned it to her holster beneath her suede russet-colored jacket. She wore her badge under her shirt. The jacket would cover her service weapon from sight and she just felt more comfortable with the weapon near at hand.

Before Kee's call, Ava had broken into the tribe's clinic, which she knew was due to reopen this week. As she suspected, all their files were digitized and the computers password-protected. Kee's and Hauser's passwords had been easy to discern, but the clinic's was a different story. So much for that plan, she thought. Shifting approaches, she'd placed a hidden camera directly over the administrator's desk. Then she could remotely activate the camera, which had a six-hour battery. But then she had to wait for the clinic to open and for Betty Mills to log in before Ava could gain access to their system.

She wondered how long before their police discovered she was here and how long before her police force learned that she'd very definitely gone off the reservation. What she was doing could cost her her job. Her position gave her authority, respect and the autonomy she'd always longed for. She didn't want to lose all that. But she was willing to chance it because the only thing more important than being a detective was finding Louisa and saving those missing girls.

She wondered if Day's disappearance was related to this case. Suspicious things were happening and they all spun like a tornado around that clinic.

She hoped the worst thing that could've happened to Dr. Day was an accident that had left him lying along the trail somewhere with a twisted ankle and without a phone. But her gut told her that his disappearance could be related to her case.

Kidnapping a federal employee would be a terrible move and very brazen. Even if they thought he was investigating the clinic and closing in on the culprit, which he likely wasn't, it would be better to…push him off a cliff.

The thought made Ava's stomach churn.

Ava stared up at the mountain. Somewhere along that trail were several cliff dwellings. She'd never seen them but her sister, Sara, had told her about them. That also meant that there were cliffs.

Kee pulled up in his old blue pickup. He climbed down and hurried toward her, looking distracted as he greeted her by clasping both elbows and kissing her on the cheek. She was so rattled by the simple brushing of his mouth on her cheek that it wasn't until Kee was already halfway to Day's Subaru that she realized what he intended.

"Don't touch that!" she called.

He paused and turned back. "Why?"

"Umm, what if something happened to him, then wouldn't this be a crime scene?" That wasn't well-done, she thought.

Kee backed up. "A crime scene?" He looked even more agitated as he looked in through the dusty windows from a safe distance. "Everything looks normal. He didn't lock it."

"You know this trail?" asked Ava, drawing him away from the vehicle.

"Part of it. It's a quarter mile past the pasture to the lower ruins. I only hiked to the upper ruins once." He rubbed his leg and frowned. "Couldn't keep up with my kid brothers."

How hard that must have been, always being the slowest, Ava thought. She touched his cheek with the palm of her hand.

"Well, you can keep up now."

They shared a smile and she resisted the urge to step closer. His hands went to her waist and she moved away, not wanting him to discover her service weapon.

"There's miles of trails up there," he pointed to the ridgeline against the crystal blue sky. "And cliff dwellings, several. I suppose Richard could have tried to bike it."

From the distance she heard a low rumble.

Kee turned toward the road. "That will be Ty. You know about him?"

She had run his record but she didn't say that. Instead she offered a half-truth. "I mentioned meeting you to my sister. And…"

Kee flushed. "She naturally mentioned Ty and… my father, too?"

She nodded, wondering why he looked so ashamed. *He* hadn't robbed a store. Mr. Perfect, she thought again. No missteps except the ones of his family reflecting badly on him. The law didn't judge families; it judged individuals. She did the same. But she knew the pain caused by the poor decisions made by family members. Her mother had been a train wreck and Sara had gotten pregnant in high school. It happened.

"No one is perfect," she said.

"I'm not like my dad." He met her gaze and she thought the expression was not shame but anger. Was he angry at his father for being a con or at her sister for gossiping? "I've never broken a law in my life."

She'd have to see about that.

"In fact, seeing my dad's sentencing, well, it changed me. I'd always been cautious because of my leg. But that made me realize that your reputation, well, it's more breakable than bones."

She thought about how one wrong step and her own reputation would be beyond repair. She had a stellar law enforcement career, but even that wouldn't survive the fallout of her rogue investigation if she was caught. But wasn't Louisa's life worth that?

The distinctive sound of a powerful engine brought all heads about.

"That's his chopper," said Kee.

"Harley?" she asked, raising her voice as the rumble became a roar.

"Indian," he said. "Wait. That's a new bike."

Ty made an entrance. Up until today, Ava had only heard about him. The family black sheep, currently under investigation for his role in the abduction of Kacey Doka. They had statements from both his youngest brother, Colt, and Kacey, but neither could testify as they were in witness protection. The signed statements implicating Ty in Kacey Doka's kidnapping from the clinic should be enough to convict him in tribal court. So why were they letting him run around free?

The roar grew louder and Ava had to shout to be heard.

"Isn't he bringing the dog?" she asked.

Kee nodded and pointed. In rolled Ty Redhorse on a coffee-brown-and-cream Harley Davidson motorcycle laden with so much chrome she could see reflections of the sky and road and man all at once.

At first she thought he was riding double, and he was, after a fashion. The dog sat behind him, paws on his shoulders, with goggles on his massive head. As Ty pulled forward, she could see the shepherd sat in a bucket fixed to the rear seat and wore some sort of restraining belt.

The engine idled and Ty fixed his stare on them both. No smile, she realized, and he looked less than pleased to be here. Ty's hair was shoulder length and cut blunt. He resembled Kee but for the cleft in his chin. He also sent all her cop senses into high alert. That challenge in his eyes as he met her gaze would have made her pull him over if she had her cruiser.

Badass didn't cover it. And he wore black, of course.

Ava regarded the dog, with its lolling, pink tongue and—what appeared to be—a wide grin.

"Looks like a wolf," said Ava.

"German shepherd mix," said Kee.

"Mixed with wolf," she said and Kee laughed.

The deep masculine rumble did crazy things to her insides.

"Ty thinks it's funny because he's riding with his bi…" Kee changed his mind about what he was going to say and motioned to Ava. "Shall we?"

Ty rocked the bike onto its kickstand. He greeted Kee with a bear hug that nearly lifted Kee off his feet. Ty was taller, broader and more intimidating.

Kee had a cell phone clipped to his clean, fitted jeans and he wore a blue button-up shirt with a turquoise bolo and brown lace-up shoes. Ty had a knife clipped to his leather belt and had a wallet connected to a belt loop by a stainless-steel chain. He wore black leather chaps over jeans, high moccasins with the distinctive toe-tab marking them as Apache footwear and a black muscle shirt that revealed a tribal tattoo circling each arm. What he didn't wear was a helmet.

She watched Ty stroke his dog's pointed ear, momentarily bending it flat before releasing her from the bucket-style pet transporter. The dog came forward to sniff Kee and then turned to Ava. She extended her hand, but the dog stopped short of her and dropped to all fours, lying alert before her.

She glanced first to Kee and then to Ty, who was narrowing his eyes at her.

Kee made introductions but Ty remained where he was. Her skin prickled a warning. She was made. She knew it.

Ty gave her a hard look.

"She a cop?" he asked Kee.

She narrowed her eyes, wondering if it was her appearance or his dog that had tipped him off.

"No," said Kee. "A neighbor."

"You packing?" he asked.

She nodded and showed her sidearm.

Ty's eyes narrowed and Kee gaped.

"You can't carry a weapon here," said Kee.

Ty held her gaze a long while and Kee shifted restlessly. Finally, he broke the silence.

"We brought something of Richard's for Hemi," said Kee. "Let me get it." He retrieved a pair of gray bike riding gloves.

Kee offered them to Ty and Ava noted that his younger brother was a few inches taller than Kee, but likely hadn't been originally. The surgeries had taken three inches from his healthy leg.

Ty took the gloves and offered them to Hemi. The dog stood and was all business when she checked out the neoprene gloves and then lowered her head to the ground, making straight for the Subaru.

She jumped so that she stood on her back legs, with her front paws pressed to the door.

"Good girl," said Ty, in a tone that seemed out of place from such a tough character. It gave her hope that he might be more than he appeared, because he appeared to be a gang member. But he had come at Kee's request and that allowed her to continue to operate covertly.

Ty waved his dog toward the trail.

"Track," he said.

Hemi put her nose to the ground and bounded away straight for the path that cut through the pasture toward the lower ruins.

Ty used Richard's gloves to wipe away the paw prints from the Subaru. Ava's eyes narrowed. Clearly, he suspected foul play and was removing evidence of Hemi's contact with the vehicle. Was he just keeping his involvement secret or did he have something to hide?

They headed up the trail with Hemi darting ahead. She fell in beside Kee.

Kee asked Ty about Colt, how he was doing and if he was still talking. Ty paused to give him a long inscrutable look and then told Kee that he was but failed to mention that Colt was not on the rez. Kee didn't seem to know that and Ty didn't tell him.

Very odd, she thought.

"When you see him last?" asked Ty.

"The Saturday when you took him to Darabee Hospital."

Almost two weeks ago. Kee had let his work erode his connection to family. He was right here on the rez but seemed to have little idea what was happening under his nose.

"Is he getting some help?" asked Kee.

"Yeah. Lots of help."

Help relocating, thought Ava.

She had read in Ty's file that he had driven a '73 Plymouth Barracuda when he allegedly kidnapped Kacey Doka, the only girl to escape her captors. But the car was never found. No car, no physical evidence connecting Kacey Doka to Ty Redhorse. Just the statement by Kacey, who was no longer here to back it up with her physical presence during testimony in tribal court, and the tribe's council had declined the FBI's request for custody of Ty. That in itself was not unusual. Most tribes were exceedingly reluctant to allow outsiders to try their defendants. Considering the history between the Tonto Apache tribes and the federal government, few would blame them.

"What kind of a car does Ty drive?" Ava asked.

"I can't keep up," said Kee. "He changes cars like I change surgical gloves. I think he's working on a '67 Pontiac GTO."

"Fast car. What color? Black?"

"No, gold."

Gang colors, she thought. Yellow and black. Those were the colors worn by the Wolf Posse here.

So Ty was a gang member, and his brother Jake was a member of the tribal police force. Which side was Kee on?

When they reached the trailhead with the marker of regulations and the one of historical information, they paused. It delineated the rules in bullet points including no fires and no firearms.

Hemi flashed by, circling the ruins. The red stone walls still stood rising ten feet in places and in others lay as piles of rock strewn on the ground. The interior chambers of rooms that had collapsed hundreds of years ago were visible and the roof beams hung at odd angles.

Once an ancient people had lived and farmed in this place, leaving behind the remnants of these communal residences. Her people called them the ancient ones, for they were here and gone before the Apache moved into the Southwestern territory.

Funny that many Americans thought that settlement of this country began in Plymouth in 1622 when at that time this settlement of hunter-farmers was living in an ancient version of a condominium right here.

The upper ruins were even older and of a different people. The Anasazi dwelt in cliffs and the whys of that were still mysterious. A drought? A new enemy? All that was known was what they had left behind.

"How many cliff dwellings up there?" she asked.

"Four, I think. More tucked all over the ridges around here."

Hemi was now on the move toward the winding path that led to the upper ruins.

Ava knew that the tribal museum gave guided tours to these two archeological sites twice a week or by arrangement. She had never seen either, but she had seen ones like it.

They hiked for thirty minutes up a steep trail. She saw tire tracks in the sandy places consistent with a bike tire. Her thigh muscles burned from the strenuous hike. She wondered how anyone could bike such a thing. The sweat on her body dried in the arid air, making her wish she had brought water.

Hemi disappeared and then reappeared, checking on the progress of the slow-moving humans. They found her, at last sitting beside an expensive-looking mountain bike that lay on its side.

"That's not good," said Ty.

"That's his," said Kee, studying the bike with worried eyes. He reached and then stopped himself.

She was glad because she didn't want to talk like a cop in front of Ty.

Ty glanced at Hemi, who lay with her paws outstretched toward the bike.

"Trail ends here," said Ty.

"Definitely?" asked Kee.

Ty glanced at Hemi, her tongue lolling as his dog looked to him for further instructions.

"It ends here or goes where Hemi can't follow."

They all stepped past the bike to look over the cliff. Below were rocks and trees but no obvious sign of Dr. Day.

"Might have fallen," said Ty.

"With his bike way over there?" she asked. That didn't seem right.

"Stopped to take in the view. Lost his footing." Ty shrugged.

Was he trying to sell her on this scenario?

"Either way, he's not here," said Kee. "We should call Jake."

Ty backed away. "If you're calling tribal, I'm gone. They're already trying to hang me for giving Kacey a ride. They'll tie me up in this, too."

A ride? Is that what he called kidnapping? Ava could not keep from gaping.

Kee stared at Ty. "What are you talking about?" *Didn't Kee know?*

Ty had been detained for questioning and released. He had not been arrested or charged. Tribal police would keep such matters private particularly if there was an ongoing investigation. She knew of Ty's situation only because her chief had been told of a possible connection to the tribe's gang and a known associate, Ty Redhorse. But the police here had taken steps to be certain Ty's detention remained secret. She knew he was a suspect but Kee did not, which meant that his brother had not told him. Ty did not want Kee to know. Was Ty protecting him or hanging him out to dry?

Ty shook his head. "Just tell them you found the car and followed the trail. That you know he bikes this route and you were checking. But I was never here. Got it?"

Kee's mouth was tight. "You want me to lie to the police?"

"Omit," said Ty.

"It's lying."

"Hey, you do what you want. Just don't call me for help again." He turned to Ava and gave her a two-finger salute. "Officer."

Then he disappeared back down the trail. Hemi followed, venturing out before him.

Kee turned to her immediately. "Why did he call you—"

"What's that?"

Ava spotted a tiny speck of canary yellow visible between the treetops below the cliff upon which they stood.

Exactly the color Kee said Dr. Day had been wearing.

Chapter Four

Ava didn't think Kee had pushed Richard Day, but she kept him in front of her on the descent. When they reached the bottom of the trail it was nearly six at night. The sun had disappeared behind the opposite ridgeline and the colors were gradually fading all around them. Kee tried tribal police but there was no cell service out here. He offered Ava the last of the water he carried and she took a long swallow before returning the empty bottle.

"You know it will be really dark soon. We have thirty minutes," she said.

"Maybe we should go to the police."

Yeah, except she was certain how Detective Jack Bear Den or the chief of police would respond if they knew where her personal leave from her soon-to-be previous job had taken her.

She'd interviewed. Been hired here, and Tinnin himself had briefed her about her first case. This case. The missing women from Turquoise Canyon, but he did not know that the last girl taken was Ava's niece. The niece that she had helped raise. So Ava was not playing by the rules on this investigation. So for now, she couldn't let either of those men see her. Not yet.

"We could find him," she coaxed. "He's maybe

ten minutes in that direction. It will be harder in the dark."

Kee hesitated, glancing in the direction of the lot. She gave one final push. "What if he's alive?"

That set him in motion. She pushed back the admiration. Kee seemed kind and conscientious and really sweet. But appearances could be deceiving.

"Do you know if anyone would want to hurt him?" she asked.

"No. I don't. He's only been here since early October. You think it's him, don't you?"

"You said he was wearing yellow."

Kee looked back along the trail. The sky still held a few bands of orange but that wouldn't last.

"I don't think anyone could survive such a fall." He looked to her. "How can you be so calm?"

Because she'd seen death before, too many times.

"We should hurry," she said, motioning. "Have you seen anyone strange around lately?"

"Outsiders?"

"Yeah. At the clinic or speaking to Day or maybe just in your neighborhood?"

"We only treat tribal members."

Kee drew up short. "It's him."

Ava came alongside him. It was a body, battered and bloody, and wearing yellow spandex that seemed to glow with unnatural brightness in the twilight.

Ava had seen bodies in worse shape. Mostly natural causes, left inside a hot trailer for days before anyone went to check, and then there were the auto accidents. But her reservation was small and relatively quiet and flat. No one fell off anything high and she was not prepared for the damage to Dr. Day.

His body had clearly struck the rock face on the descent and possibly some of the tall pines, judging from the deep lacerations on his torso and thigh. There were branches and debris surrounding him. He lay on his stomach with his arms and legs sprawled as if he were about to use a horizontal Stairmaster.

Kee knelt beside his roommate and checked his carotid pulse, but Ava knew from the brownish stain on Day's cornea and the pooling of blood in the lower half of his face that Day was gone.

Her Apache heritage included all sorts of beliefs that it was dangerous to touch the dead. That ghosts could follow you even if the deceased was a good friend in life. Ava didn't believe that dead bodies and ghosts could haunt her but she dearly hoped that whoever did this would be haunted because she was certain Day had not fallen. He'd been pushed. That was her theory and she was going with it.

She swept the body with her gaze, looking for clues, and found them right there in Day's hand. His nails were torn and bloody and there was skin and hair under them. That was what you'd see if Day had fought his attacker. So whoever pushed him would have scratches on their face or arms. Maybe both.

Ava tried to think of a way to take a sample from his nails.

"I have to call Hector," said Kee.

That was an odd first call, she thought. Why not to Jake, his brother who was on the force?

He looked at Ava with wide, troubled eyes and swallowed, sending his Adam's apple bobbing. "He's our medical examiner."

Of course he was, she thought.

Kee rocked back on his heels and wiped his mouth with his hand, looking truly unsettled. Rattled, she corrected. She knew he had faced death. All physicians did. But this death was harder. He knew the man, so it was personal. Day was young and he had been Kee's colleague plus they'd shared a FEMA trailer. Add to that the damage to the corpse and you had a horror that would not soon be forgotten.

She dropped to a knee beside Kee and draped an arm around his shoulders. Kee clasped her hand with his opposite one.

"Look at his nails," she said and pointed.

"What is that?" He leaned closer.

"Looks like skin."

Kee straightened and stepped quickly away. She watched him pace, both hands locked behind his head. Finally, he came back beside her.

"You think he was pushed. You think he fought his attacker."

"Don't you?"

He nodded gravely.

"Should you take a sample?" she asked.

He shook his head. "The police will do that. I'll make sure they do."

"What about photos?" she asked. The scene might not be so pristine later on and it would be dark. She did not want to use her phone knowing that it would be confiscated as evidence and that would give the police here easy access to who she was. But those photos could be vital.

"Should I take some?" He had his phone out.

"Might help your police."

Kee took a few shots, his mouth squeezed in a look of distaste. She nudged him to photograph Day's hands, face and all other injuries. Finally she suggested a few long shots of the scene.

"Might help with location," she said, knowing it would. He finished and his arm dropped to his side with the glowing phone gripped in his hand. He stood staring at Day as if he could not believe what he was seeing.

She slipped her hand into the crook of his elbow and he jumped.

"You want to see if you have cell service here?" she asked.

He placed his hand over hers and rubbed as if to give her comfort. "Doubtful. But I'll try."

Kee lifted the phone, searching for a signal.

"Nothing."

"Come on," she said. "We'll go tell the police what we found. You can lead them back here."

Kee stood over the body, head bowed as if he were a mourner at a grave.

"I was afraid something like this had happened," he said.

Ava's antenna picked up. It was the sort of thing a person who knew what would happen would say.

"Why is that?" she asked, keeping her tone conversational.

"He was gone too long." Kee glanced back toward the body, arms folded protectively before him. "He was going to get a haircut after work today."

Now, that was the kind of crazy thing people did say when someone was ripped unexpectedly from their life.

She didn't like to admit it, but her opinions as to Kee's involvement were eroding. Ava had an instructor in the academy who told her students to keep a few brain cells open to the possibility that your prime suspect was innocent. Those brain cells were recruiting others and that troubled her. What if she was wrong about Dr. Redhorse? If she were, then she needed to expand her search or target his fellow doctor more closely. It just seemed with his brother Ty's involvement and his brother Colt's disappearance into witness protection without Kee's knowledge that the tribe considered Kee a prime suspect. Ava was unsettled and she did not like the uncertainty growing within her.

They walked back using their phone flashlights to help illuminate the trail. Once at the cars they paused. Ava needed to not be here when the police arrived.

"Listen, I'd like to get home. My sister has a thing at the school tonight and if I'm there she can cancel the sitter." An AA meeting that Sara had promised to attend. "The girls are more anxious since Louisa's disappearance." Ava shrugged. "So how about this, I'll call the police when I get cell service and send them back to you. Okay?"

Kee frowned. "I'm sure they'll want to speak to you."

"Yes, I'll be at my sister's. They can come there. Better if it's after nine. Kids in bed." She shrugged.

"All right. I'll tell them." He clasped her arm and she felt the strength of his hands as he leaned in. "You be okay walking back alone?"

"Yes. I'll be fine." She tried and failed not to let his concern affect her. Ava smiled and met his warm gaze, feeling the unwelcome stirring of attraction thread between them.

"Thank you, for everything."

On impulse, Ava lifted to her toes and planted a kiss on his cheek.

Kee's mouth dropped open and his hand slipped away. She'd surprised him. She took the opportunity to make her escape.

She did call the police, did not give her name, pretending she was upset by events, and sent help in Kee's direction. They had her number, of course, but there was no need to track it unless they could not find her. If she was lucky, she had a day or two of anonymity left.

AVA GOT BACK to her sister's place around eight. Woody greeted her with much enthusiasm and she let him out. Her sister was sprawled on the couch and did not move as Ava closed the door. Her snores and the beer cans covering the coffee table told her all she needed to know. Beyond her sister's unconscious body sat the kitchen table on which lay various plastic containers and a greasy red-and-white-striped paper bucket from the fast-food chicken place in Darabee.

She would deal with Sara later; right now she wanted to check on the girls. She continued down the narrow hallway of the trailer to the first, smaller bedroom. Inside, all the girls sat on the lower bunk with their eyes fixed on the television as avatars danced in bright colors across the screen. The twins, Alexandra and Margarita, held the controls while Olivia watched the screen. Margarita glanced up at her return and offered a weak smile before her gaze cut back to the game. Ava nodded to her and returned the smile. Then she shut off the TV. The controls that Alexandra and Margarita held sagged as they groaned in unison.

"You all get some supper?" she asked, stroking Olivia's soft hair.

The chorus of yeses followed.

"Homework?"

Their eyes glanced here and there but did not meet hers.

"Kitchen table. Now. Bring your work."

The groans were unanimous but they dragged their backpacks to the table as Ava cleared away the remains of the take-out meal. The girls drew out their school workbooks and Ava cut up the apples she had purchased. To this she added celery filled with peanut butter and raw broccoli and ranch dressing.

Woody scratched on the front door and Ava let him in. He settled under the table at the girls' feet.

Ava gave Olivia paper and a large pencil so she could doodle while her sisters worked on tracing letters of the alphabet. Margarita was excellent at counting and needed no help. But neither girl could do the matching of Tonto words to pictures of animals.

"Mom doesn't speak to us in Apache," said Margarita.

Ava switched to Tonto Apache and determined that she would use more of their native language from here on. Who they were, their culture and their heritage included their language.

The girls ate everything but the broccoli. Well, it was worth a try.

She told them in Tonto that it was bedtime and they understood that well enough to protest.

"Mom sleeps a lot," said Olivia.

Ava thought of the promise her sister had made to seek help. Yet here Sara was, drunk with such young children in the house. How could she be so irresponsible and give up control like that? It made Ava sad and angry all at once.

She had them in their beds before nine thirty. Since her arrival, the twins shared the top bunk, giving Ava the lower one. Olivia slept in the other bedroom with her mom but had crept in to sleep with Ava on two occasions, so tonight Ava just put her to bed in the lower bunk.

Ava drew the covers up around Margarita and Alexandra, who shared the top one. Then she kissed each girl good-night.

Olivia had the covers drawn up to her chin when Ava stooped to kiss her on the forehead.

"I'm glad you're here," said Margarita.

"Me, too."

"Can you stay?" Alexandra asked her aunt.

"For a while."

Alexandra rolled to her side, giving Ava her back. She didn't blame the girl. Her father had left by dying. Her big sister was taken and her mother was here but still gone. It filled Ava with a bone-deep sadness. She stroked Margarita's shoulder and whispered good-night in Tonto. From the door she flicked off the light but left the hall light on, as they preferred.

Back in the trailer's living room she helped her sister rise from the couch.

"Diamond?" she muttered, her husband's name.

That cut through Ava. She knew how much her sister missed him. But it made her angry, too, because she did not want these girls bounced around like rubber balls. Why couldn't Sara pull herself together?

"It's Ava," she said, drawing her sister's arm around hers.

"Ava? What are you doing here?"

"I've been here a week."

"Where are the girls?"

"In their room. Sara, you promised you'd go to that meeting tonight."

"What meeting?"

Ava sighed and continued toward her sister's room.

She got her sister to the bedroom, where she sat, head bowed. At first, Ava thought Sara had fallen asleep again, but then she saw her shoulders shake and heard the familiar sound of her sister's weeping.

"Louisa," she whispered and covered her face with her hands.

Ava sat on the bed beside her sister and pulled her in. Sara collapsed against her, clinging to her shirt. Ava hugged her tight, cradling her older sister to her chest.

"We're going to get her back, Sara. I swear to God, we are."

Chapter Five

Sara and the girls had fallen asleep when the knock for Ava came on her door. It was a young police officer whom she had not met on her interviews. He identified himself as Officer Daniel Wetselline.

She motioned him in and got him a cup of coffee. He asked her all the questions he should have asked her for a preliminary round interview, scribbling on his pad as he drank his coffee.

Ava wondered how long before someone at tribal realized that Ava Hood was Avangeline Hood Yokota, their new hire from the Saguaro Flat Apache Tribe?

"And you were the one who discovered the body?"

"I found his car based on information provided by Dr. Redhorse. From the cliff I saw something bright yellow. But Dr. Redhorse and I discovered the body together."

Wetselline nodded, showing that this answer agreed with what he had already heard. She'd have to talk to him about that. It was bad practice to let witnesses or suspects know what you thought you already knew.

He finished his coffee and then thanked her for her time. She walked him to the door. He asked her to stop by the station tomorrow to meet with the investigating detective, Jack Bear Den.

She saw him out just before eleven. She closed the door behind him and resisted the urge to sag against the trailer door.

Woody sat before her, staring soulfully up into her eyes, his thick balding tail thumping against the linoleum tile.

"No one took you for a walk today. Did they?"

His eyebrows lifted.

"No, I didn't think so."

Ava slipped into a fleece jacket and took Woody out on a leash. Lots of folks let their dogs roam around the rez, but she'd seen family pets stalked and attacked by wild dogs, so she didn't take chances. Woody wasn't used to the restraint and tugged her along in his hurry to get from one interesting smell to the next.

When they reached Kee's trailer she noticed the light. She paused, thinking of him, home from the crime scene in the trailer he had shared with Richard Day. If he were innocent, it would be a tough night. Her feeling was that he might not know what was happening. She didn't yet know, either. But she believed that whatever it was, it centered on the tribe's health clinic.

She considered knocking on his front door when she noticed the light from the back of the trailer. She and Woody walked along between the trailers. She smelled the sweet scent of a citronella candle.

She took another step toward the back, rounding the trailer at the same time she spotted the triple flame in the large candle set in a tin bucket perched on the side table between two folding chairs. Kee sat in one, speaking to someone in the second chair. In the light of the candle's flame she could not make out the identity of the occupant.

She stepped closer and saw that the second man was Dr. Hector Hauser. There they sat, prime suspects, number one and two. Ava had gone as far as she could checking out Kee. The desire to meet Hauser was irresistible.

She held her position, pressing her elbow against her side and feeling the reassuring bulge of her service pistol in her shoulder holster. She unzipped her jacket.

"Hello?" she called.

Both men spun in their chairs.

Woody led her forward into the meager candlelight.

"Who's that?" said Hauser.

Woody was now wagging his tail and tugging at the leash.

"Woody?" said Kee.

"Yes, that's him," she said and allowed him to pull her into the light.

"Ava!" Kee was on his feet and approaching, hands out to greet her. "We were just talking about you."

That, of course, made her ears go back. She didn't

want to be the subject of conversation, especially not between these two men.

"Come here," he said. His wide grin made it seem as if he were delighted to see her. "I want you to meet Hector."

Dr. Hauser was now on his feet. She knew him very well, but he had never laid eyes on her. She'd been very careful to be certain of that. But the time for surveillance was past. She needed to stir the pot.

He didn't look like a monster, either.

Hauser's curious eyes raked her with a quick down and up glance as he offered his hand to the dog. He did not offer his hand to her, however, except to lift it in the old style of greeting. She found herself checking his arms and face for any sign of recent injury and found none visible. But he wore a light jacket against the chill. The temperature dropped at night more quickly here than down on the flats.

Kee made formal introductions. That provided Dr. Hauser with enough information that he might be able to discover who she was if he was looking. Ava tried and failed to ignore the cold chill that raced down her spine.

Dr. Hauser greeted her formally in Tonto Apache. She responded in kind and he asked her a few simple questions in Apache.

"You are visiting your sister?" he asked in Tonto.

"Yes, for two weeks."

"Then back to your home?" he asked.

"That is what I intend. Yes."

"Kee tells me you do not yet have a husband."

She held her smile. "This is true."

Hauser turned to Kee and switched to English. "She speaks our language beautifully." He nodded in approval as he turned to her. "Good to see that they teach their children well down on Saguaro."

"Well, I learned at school, but also from my grandmother."

"Very good. Please take my seat. I was just leaving."

"Oh, don't leave on my account. I'm just taking Woody for a walk. I need to get back."

"Isn't your sister at home?" asked Hauser.

"Yes, but…" She wasn't offering information about her sister's condition, but she feared she already had.

"Ah," said Hauser. "I see. Well, she has suffered two great losses. It is understandable, her grief."

He held his smile.

Ava did not think that drinking and grieving were the same thing, but she only murmured her agreement.

Hauser clapped Kee on the shoulder and then turned to Ava.

"Nice to meet you, Ava Hood." He offered a farewell in Tonto and headed off.

"He's very big on learning our language," said Kee.

"I see that."

Why hadn't she seen Hauser's car?

"Did he walk here?" she asked. It was over a mile between Kee's trailer and Hauser's.

"Yes, why?"

She shook her head.

"It's not too far. Hector doesn't sleep well and we all are reeling over what has happened."

Hauser didn't seem to be reeling. He seemed… content. And now he had her name, most of it. Things were about to get interesting.

"Come and sit. Can I get you something? I have vitamin water and tap water." His smile left him and he glanced around as if he'd misplaced something.

Woody went to him and nuzzled his hand. Kee stroked his head absently.

"We got ahold of Day's family. His parents. He wasn't married."

He offered the chair and she sat. He drew his chair up close to hers. His feet were bare and his button-up shirt flapped open. His hair was wet and he smelled like something spicy and enticing. Why was she here again?

She glanced at the three empty beer bottles on the table.

"You drinking?" she asked.

"Yup. Ice tea. You going to turn me in?"

Warning bells rang in her mind. Turn him in? Did he know who she was? He'd given no indication. Ty suspected. Had Ty called Kee? She was certain that Jake Redhorse had not tipped him, because she and Jake had not met on her visits to her soon-to-be new police force. Tribal police didn't expect her until November 1, and by then she planned to have her niece back if she didn't get killed or fired before then. Besides, with what she was doing, it was better all around if she was not affiliated with either force.

"For what?"

"Drinking caffeine past bedtime. I couldn't sleep, so…" He motioned to the yard.

"What about your boss? He drop by often?"

"No, but tonight… Well, just checking in."

Because his roommate had just died or was he checking up? She suspected that either Kee or Hauser or both of them were tied up in the recent disappearances. She wanted it to be Hauser and not Kee.

But for that to all be happening under Kee's nose, it was unlikely, despite his obvious hero worship of Hauser. The man was not a hero. Heroes didn't cheat on their wives, which she'd already found out about. What other secrets was he harboring?

She made a sound in her throat. "It's been a hard day."

"Yet you don't seem rattled."

"I didn't know him."

"But at the car, waiting by yourself and then on the trail with Ty, you were so calm. And at the body." He waved his hand at the sky. "You weren't even fazed? Why is that?"

He was too damn smart.

"Most folks I know would go out of their way not to see what we saw today," he continued. "I know I'll have nightmares. Finding a body, my roommate." He grimaced. "It's a different way of seeing death. What about you, Ava?"

She needed him off this line of questioning. She slipped her hand into his. His brows rose in surprise.

"Hector seems nice."

He shook his head. "Tonight he was on again about how I need to settle down. Fill that big house I'll have with babies." He gave her an assessing stare and now she was the one rattled.

"What house?"

He told her about the perks of working for the clinic. She managed not to look completely stunned. Her clinic had a doctor out of medical school and a tribe member who was a nurse practitioner. The doctors came and went as they moved on and up.

She turned in her seat.

"Is that what you want? A wife and lots of babies."

The way he held her gaze made her insides quicken. His slow smile only increased her breathing rate. "Eventually. But not because I have an extra bedroom. I've seen a lot of unwanted children born. I think every child born should be wanted."

She could not disagree.

She squeezed his hand, trying and failing not to notice the heat generated by his palm pressed to hers. Only afterward did she start thinking of who the unwanted children he was referring to might be. Did he mean the missing girls? The ones from big, troubled families?

"You must have had some opportunities, some women or a woman," she said.

"A few."

His smile was charming and his face, well, it was the kind of face she knew she would never grow tired of. Why did he have to be tied up in this? In other circumstances, he would be just the sort of man she would find appealing because he was so different than the jaded, sarcastic law enforcement officers that filled her world. Maybe it was because Kee got to save people. He wasn't exposed to the kind of human wreckage witnessed by police officers.

"Yet no one has managed to tag and bag the doctor?" she asked.

His smile vanished and he redirected his gaze away from her.

"You know, that's just it. I've been made to feel like an eight-point buck in hunting season. Women down there in Phoenix, well, they were definitely on the hunt." He looked away. "There was one woman. I almost married her."

"Almost?"

He sank back in his chair, legs thrust out in front of him. "Once we got engaged she got very pushy. Wanted to spend money on the wedding and a honeymoon in Fiji, and meanwhile I was eating mac and cheese from a box. I tried to explain that not all doctors make big bucks and none at first but…"

"You broke up with her?"

"She broke up with me. Married a dentist."

"Ouch."

"Better off. I felt hurt but mostly relieved."

"Lots of reasons to want to marry a doctor, I suppose," she said. She ticked them off. "Security, status, bragging rights over all your girlfriends and let's not forget the money."

"Not all doctors earn high salaries."

"Better than cops," she said.

He gave her a puzzled look and she smiled, trying to cover her slip.

"Your brother is a police officer. Right?"

"Oh, yeah."

"What about you, Ava. Those things important to you? Bragging rights and all?"

She met his gaze and saw the humor she had used had not transferred to him. He looked sad and wary.

"First off, I don't need a man to define who I am. Second, I like my independence and third, I don't think I'd like being married to a doctor, especially an emergency medicine doctor."

"Why?"

"You're like cops. You see all the bad stuff and it makes you either cynical or overly cautious."

"I've always been cautious."

"Why is that?"

He shrugged. "Mostly my leg problems. Fragile bones during the time when most young men are crashing into people and things on purpose."

"Sports?"

"Not for me. Plus it stresses me out to break the rules. I've never been pulled over by police. Not even a traffic ticket. I set my cruise control five miles below the limit. I wear my safety belt. Look before I leap and spend way too much time thinking through decisions."

In other words, he was the opposite of Ty, who tested the limits and broke rules consistently, and Jake, who took chances just by virtue of his job.

He pressed a hand to the top of his head and blew out a long breath.

"Sound kind of—"

"Boring?" he asked.

"Unexpected."

"I'm not like my brothers. Colt and Ty went off to defend their country. Jake swore to protect and serve."

"And you swore to do no harm."

He smiled. "Yes."

Ava was beginning to doubt that Kee was the sort of man capable of taking those girls. And if she could clear him she could...

Bad idea, Ava. He could be playing you.

As if on cue, Kee said, "So, what kind of a man do you like?"

Chapter Six

Ava was tempted to say she liked the sort of man that stuck around. She'd never met her father and her grandfather had died when she was two. The closest thing Ava had to a man she could rely on was her drill sergeant and that was just sad.

"Kee, listen, if you're asking because you're interested, I'll tell you right off that I don't have a great track record with men. I tend to bail when they get possessive."

"Why?"

"Independence, again."

"Why is independence more important to you than a committed relationship?"

"Committed?" She laughed. "Well, I haven't seen too many of them." But she had been on her share of domestic disturbance calls.

"Your parents? They still together?"

Wow. Right to the heart of her personal chaos.

"My mom got pregnant young. The boy, my older sister's dad, left the rez right after he found out Mom was pregnant because he was nineteen and she was only sixteen. Mom dropped out and moved back in with my grandparents. She had me three years later..." She turned to face him.

"I can't believe you're twenty-eight. Honestly, you look barely old enough to order a drink."

"Don't I know it. I get proofed a lot."

The smile they shared lingered far too long. Ava broke the contact of their gaze.

"So you lived with your mom and grandmother," he prompted, then waited.

"You sure you want to hear this?"

He nodded. "Go on."

"So after I was born Mom ran off with the boy. Left me with her mother. My grandmother raised us until I was eight."

"Then your mom came back?"

She snorted. There he was, searching for a happy ending.

"Yes, because my grandmother was sick and then she died shortly afterward. My sister and I lived with my mom until… You don't need to hear this. Let's just say I had really good reasons to learn how to take care of myself."

"Your mom still around?"

"Died of liver cancer after contracting hepatitis C."

As a doctor, Kee could make some educated guesses on how her mom got sick. His silence was telling.

"Yeah, she was in court-ordered rehab. She broke the rules and was in prison so off to foster care for us again."

"I'm so sorry."

"Don't be. What doesn't kill you makes you stronger. Right?"

"I'm not sure about that."

"Yeah, well, so anyway, if you're asking about male role models, mine sucked."

"Sounds like neither of our dads got the nod to win father of the year."

"True that."

They sat in silence divided by their thoughts and the flickering candlelight. Why did she feel like she could talk about her family to Kee?

"My dad was a small-time thief," said Kee. "Not a good one. He had several convictions on the rez. Too many. Then he dragged one of my younger brothers into a big mess. Had him driving the getaway car. He was only seventeen. It was my father's third strike and the tribe turned him over to the district attorney for prosecution. He's still in prison down in Phoenix. Used to visit him when I was in medical school. He has served six of a ten-year sentence. With luck he'll stay in until my sister Abbie is grown. He's not a nice man, Ava. And my brother was arrested with him and narrowly avoided being tried as an adult."

"Ty?"

"Good guess. Yes, that was Ty. They let him join the military and avoid jail time."

She tried to think of the next logical question. Should she ask about Ty, knowing what happened to him? Or about his dad or just commiserate?

"So, I know something about bad role models," said Kee. "My father was an excellent one for what not to do. Don't steal. Don't drag your son into a gang. Don't hit your wife."

"He was physically abusive?"

"Sometimes, when my father was on a tear, we'd all take cover. But not Ty." Kee shook his head. "I don't want to talk about it. I just wanted you to know. I understand being trapped in a difficult situation. My way out was school. Ty joined the Marines. Jake joined the police and Colt…"

"He's your youngest brother?"

"He's living up in the woods like a hermit. He won't talk to anyone but Ty. He was always our lost boy, but when he came back from the US Marines he was different."

Ava couldn't keep the surprise from showing. Colt was no longer up on Turquoise Ridge but instead in witness protection. Didn't Kee even know that?

"Colt was a POW, captured. Every one of his team was tortured and killed. Ty told me that. Colt got a psych discharge. Ty got him to the clinic and I saw him there. We got him as far as Darabee Hospital, but he didn't stay. Checked himself out. He's all messed up because his girl came back."

Kacey Doka. The only one to escape captivity.

"Isn't that a good thing?" Ava asked.

"She came back pregnant with someone else's kid. Just what he needs. And now that baby will grow up without a father, too." Kee was shaking his head.

He was either the best actor in the world or he had no idea what was happening.

"When did you see Colt last?" She just had to ask.

"About a week ago. Saturday last, the seventh. But he won't speak to me."

That was only a few days before Ty allegedly took Kacey to the Russians. It was also before Colt and Kacey agreed to witness protection. This reinforced her belief that neither Ty nor Colt had told Kee. Was it possible he'd had his head down with all the extra work after the dam collapse, the injuries, the clinic's temporary move that he had missed what was happening in his family? Before the FEMA trailers, Kee had lived in his mother's home. Ava was reasonably certain that May Redhorse knew her baby boy was gone. She added this to her list of information to run down.

"Well, that's a lot to deal with." She tried not to show her confusion. "Is your mom still alone?"

"Divorced and remarried. This one is a great guy. Not terribly ambitious but a nice man. Treats her well."

Ava smiled. The man in question was Burt Rope. He had no priors.

"Well, it's late." She sat forward and he followed. "I just came by to see how you were doing. Ask you if you needed anything."

He smiled and laced his fingers with hers and then brought her hand to his lips. The dry heat of his mouth pressed to her skin, setting off a tingle of awareness and a sharp stab of need.

He drew back but kept hold of her hand. She felt the firm grasp and thought of the weapon that she had holstered just a few inches from the place where her palm pressed to his. She was safe.

"I also wanted to tell you that I'm sorry we missed our dinner tonight," she said.

His smile dropped away and he released her.

"Tuesday! Today. Ava, I'm so sorry. I forgot."

"Weren't you at the police station tonight?" she asked.

"Yes. Did they speak to you?"

She nodded.

"Could we try again? I need it, you know, with all that is going on. Tomorrow will be rough because of the autopsy."

She sat forward, all the lethargy and warm fuzzy gone as she scented prey. How convenient for Hauser to be the MDI. As the Medical Death Investigator he could put whatever he wanted as the cause of death.

"Since Dr. Hauser is doing the autopsy, I'll have to cover the clinic alone," said Kee. "Richard's family doesn't want an autopsy, but you know, accidental deaths…well." His words fell off. Then he drew a long breath and launched in again, one hand on his neck. "So I have to see patients and then get things in order for transport because we will be moving back to Piñon Flats ahead of schedule."

"When?"

"Tomorrow afternoon, sometime."

She needed to get into the clinic and to Betty Mills's computer before they reopened. It would be infinitely harder to infiltrate the permanent clinic than it was the temporary FEMA one. Who could get her inside? She eyed Kee. He could but he wouldn't do it knowingly. Breaking the rules, she thought, not his thing.

"I'm sorry," he said, shaking his head apologetically. "You don't need to hear all this."

"I don't mind." She reached out and clasped his hand. "Do you need help moving to the clinic?"

"They've got people for that."

"I'd love a private tour," she pressed. "You've spoken so highly of the facility."

"Sure."

"What about tomorrow before it opens? It would be quiet."

"Except I'm needed at the FEMA clinic. Last day in the trailers. It will be just me and the nurses. We close at noon, because of the move, but it won't really be noon. You know? We are done when we see the last patient. And then we move everything out of the trailers and back to Piñon Flats. Oh, I hope I'm not too late for dinner. Could we eat late?"

"You just give me thirty minutes' notice."

"Really? That would be great."

"So the clinic in Piñon Flats is closed until Thursday?"

"We thought so. But the women's clinic opens in the morning because they have a baby transferring back from Darabee."

A baby? Ava knew that Lori Redhorse worked in the women's facility. Kee's sister-in-law might get her in.

"When does Richard's family arrive?" Ava asked.

"Not until Thursday. They're going to bring his body back up to Minnesota for burial."

"They must be heartbroken."

"Yes. Tribal council director made the call. Spared me that. But I plan to see them in Darabee. I understand they'll stay there until arrangements can be made."

"Will you be there for the autopsy?"

He cocked his head at her question and paused.

"No, just Dr. Hauser and the guy over there in Darabee Hospital. He's the ME for the county. But since Richard died on tribal lands, Hector will be there, too. Not a normal situation because he is not a member of our tribe."

"I see." That was good news, as the medical examiner for the county would be sure that things were done correctly. Unless Hector got there first and removed evidence. "Anyone from your police force be there?"

He cocked his head and regarded her for a long moment. She realized too late that it wasn't the usual sort of question.

"I don't know."

She drew out her phone and glanced at the time. "I better get home."

Kee released her hand and rose. Woody groaned and stretched, then lifted on all fours, watching them with his tail set on medium wag.

"Let me just snuff this." He blew the flames out with a single breath and she collected Woody's leash in her right hand. He fell in beside her at her left side as they meandered toward her sister's home.

The temporary trailer park was dark, with only the light from Kee's trailer to guide them. That fell away as they continued along the road under the light of a pale quarter moon. The stars seemed especially bright and the sky more a deep blue than black. How many centuries had her people stared up at the night sky? They had named all the constellations, and stars of all varieties appeared often in their art and regalia.

She kept him on her left as they walked. If she needed her pistol, she'd only have to drop the leash and reach inside her jacket. But that did put him side by side with her shoulder holster and weapon. She wondered what he thought about handguns. Most doctors were not gun people, as they spent time pulling bullets out of human bodies.

He took her hand and locked his fingers through hers.

"I'm glad you came visiting," he said.

She wondered if he meant visiting him or her sister. But it didn't matter. The moonlight and the quiet night were weaving a spell. Making her forget who she was and who he was. The darkness shrouded them, giving them the illusion of privacy and the feeling that they were the only two people here.

"So? Dinner tomorrow night?" he asked.

She smiled. "Sure."

"I'll call before I pick you up."

When they reached her sister's FEMA trailer, they drew to a halt and he turned to face her. Kee was leaning in. She looked up at him. The moon cast his face in silvery light, making his sculpted features seem to be carved of some exotic wood. His smile was gentle but his eyes glittered with unmistakable desire. Her heart kicked into high gear.

"I'm going to kiss you good-night," he said.

Warning or promise, she wondered and thought it a little of both. It was just a kiss. What harm could that do?

She lifted on her toes, meeting him halfway. He gripped her shoulders, his hands sweeping down to her elbows. And then his mouth was slanting over hers, soft at first as he explored the fit of their mouths and then harder as he cradled her head and deepened the kiss.

All her senses jumped and quivered. Her skin puckered on her arms as every hair on her skin lifted up in recognition of the powerful chemistry activated by his kiss. Ava was not without experience and that was exactly why she knew that this man, this kiss was different. Very different.

Worst choice imaginable.

But her body wasn't listening. She fell against one broad shoulder, sliding naturally into the hard plains of his chest as she relished the heat and the pressure. And she opened her mouth to let him stroke and suck and tease.

Her words echoed back to her, mocking now. *What harm could one kiss do?*

Chapter Seven

Kee felt the explosion of sensation and the building heat at the first contact of his lips to hers. His heart sped. He inhaled the sweet fragrance of her skin and felt the erotic slide of his tongue along hers. He knew the physiological reasons for each one, could describe arousal in clinical terms, but this kiss just flat-out took his words away. He could barely think, let alone speak. All he knew for certain was that he wanted more. So much more. But when his hands slid to her hips and tugged to bring them together, Ava stepped back.

He set his jaw and fixed a smile on his lips to keep her from seeing his disappointment. He'd gone too fast. He knew it and still he could not help himself. What Ava described as independent he saw as wounded. But her wounds could not be bound and healed. Not without patience and time.

He found he wanted to try, to accept that challenge if for no other reason than it might bring her to trust him enough...yes, to sleep with him. He'd admit it to himself. He wanted Ava and he was prepared to work for it just as he had worked for everything else.

"Good night, Ava. I'll see you tomorrow night."

As Kee gave Woody's head another pat, he told himself to turn around to head home. Instead he stood locked in place. He thought of his empty trailer and all that had happened and suddenly felt sad.

She blinked up at him, holding the leash, looking troubled.

"Kee?"

He gave her a smile, waiting, hoping she wasn't going to call off their dinner date.

"Will you be all right over there, you know… alone?"

"Oh, yes. I'll be okay." It wasn't an offer of anything but concern and when he'd tried to draw her against him, she'd called a halt. She was a good girl. Their culture valued modesty in both men and women. He liked that Ava didn't let him get away with too much. So far he liked everything he saw. Kee was already trying to figure out how to get her to stay in the area and he'd only met her two days ago.

His mother said it was like that sometimes. Like falling off a cliff. Kee's head dropped, thinking of Richard again.

Such a day, filled with the ordinary at the clinic and the horror of finding Richard and the wonder of kissing Ava.

She lifted on her toes and dropped a kiss on his cheek. Her mouth was warm and soft and she brought with her the enticing fragrance of earth and flowers.

Ava stepped back and made a hasty retreat,

headed for her sister's front door. Kee watched her go. Too good to be true—that had been his initial thought. Every woman he met recently was after something. Mostly when they heard that he was a doctor, their eyes lit up as if they were starving and he was dinner. He didn't get that vibe from Ava. But there was something about her that was off. She was smart, clearly, and obviously beautiful. She had a nice sense of humor and was empathetic. But her reactions to stress were just out of the ordinary. She'd have made a good paramedic with that cool head on her lovely shoulders. Seemed a waste to have her dealing cards for high rollers.

Kee headed home, glad to imagine her lying in her bed alone. It took his mind off Richard lying on a slab. He wondered what she wore to sleep as he relived their kiss. Best darn kiss he'd had in…well, forever. After he broke up with Connie, he'd buried himself in the library and had been so busy during his residency that he didn't have the time or energy for a woman. But he wanted a woman, a wife and a family. The right kind of woman, one who understood him and where he came from. Could Ava understand how much he loved and hated this place?

Could she be the one he could trust with the bad things as well as the good? Could Ava Hood be the woman who could love him for himself?

WEDNESDAY MORNING, BETTY MILLS met Hector Hauser at the temporary clinic before opening.

"I have some information from Saguaro Flats. I told them I was running a background check for employment," she said offering him the sheet. "Tribal registry shows three Ava Hoods down there. But see, this one is eighteen. This one is sixty-two. The other does work for the casino, but she's in her late forties."

Betty registered members of their tribe onto the rolls. She had connections with all of the surrounding tribes and many outside the state. A simple phone call could gain her access to information unavailable to most.

He took the page. "Hood is a common name. But why isn't she turning up?"

"That was what I wondered. So I ran just Ava. I got twenty hits. Five in the correct age range and this one…" She pointed a long acrylic nail at the paper.

Hauser read the entry. "Avangeline H. Yokota." His eyes scanned and then lowered the page to meet her eyes. "Tribal police detective?"

Betty nodded.

"Is that her?"

"I'm trying to find out if anyone knows what Sara Tah's sister does down there in Saguaro Flats. I've made some calls."

"This is bad." Hector swore in Tonto Apache. "We just had Yury here for Day. If Ava dies, as well…"

He and Betty shared a look of understanding. The

distinct-looking Russian stood out among the Tonto Apache people and would arouse suspicion if spotted. And Kee had already expressed interested in the beautiful Turquoise Canyon newcomer, which complicated plans even more.

Betty spoke first. "You do the autopsies. Just put down accidental death."

"Damn ME will be there."

"You can handle him. Day was snooping around on the computers. Trying to access my protected files. We had to take precautions."

"But why was he doing that?"

"We'll never know."

"Well, I've changed all passwords and now I get an alert if anyone accesses those files."

"Do I call him again?"

She hesitated, chewing on her knuckle.

"Wait or call the Russians?" he asked.

She dropped her hand from her mouth. "I'd err on the side of caution."

Hector lifted his mobile phone and dialed.

AVA HEADED TO tribal police headquarters in Piñon Flats just after nine on Wednesday. Autopsy was this morning and the clinic was moving today, so she figured tribal must already be set up. She was, unfortunately, right.

She had put off reporting to her soon-to-be new boss. But Day's death had changed things. She needed to be sure that neither Hauser nor Redhorse performed that autopsy. That meant coming in out of the cold. She thought she preferred the cold to the heat she was about to take. Tinnin was smart and it was better to report than let him run her to ground.

Not being affiliated with any police department gave her some leeway and, acting as a private citizen, she was involving no one but herself.

During her interview process, Tinnin had told her that they were focusing their investigation on the tribe's health clinic because all the girls had been seen there. It was the only certain connection they had yet discovered and plenty for Ava to go on. She had not told them that her main reason for applying for the position was not that she wanted a larger force, as she had told them. It was Louisa.

Tribal headquarters was unlocked and had a faint musty odor about it. She headed to the wing containing the police station and was met upon entrance by Carol Dorset, a nice older woman and longtime dispatcher for the tribe. Her face was soft and the pink lipstick she wore had bled into the wrinkles surrounding her mouth but her eyes were sharp and she recognized Ava instantly.

"We were expecting you in November," she said.

"Yes. That's right."

Carol cocked her head and waited for an explanation that Ava was not going to give her.

"We only just got back ourselves," said Carol. "Electric is back on, so tribal government, public works and the health clinic are all allowed in today and the tribal members will be allowed in on Thursday. Businesses open on Friday. Should be more folks at the diner with the construction right down the street."

"Good news," said Ava. "Is the chief busy?"

"Always. I'll tell him you're here."

Carol spoke to the chief by phone and then waved her on past the dispatch area. Ava crossed the empty squad room to the office beyond.

She found Chief Wallace Tinnin looking out of the plate-glass window at her, his phone pressed to his ear. The door was open so she stepped inside and glanced about. When she'd been here last the sideboard and desk were piled high with folders and paper. Now only the walls were cluttered with the faded photos. His desk held the phone's base and two cardboard boxes. Leaning on the near side were a pair of aluminum crutches he'd needed since breaking his foot during the dam collapse. It seemed he had not yet found time to unpack. He wore no uniform, just jeans and a pistol holstered at his hip. The gold tribal shield was clipped beside it. The desk blocked her view of his legs, but she assumed his foot was still in a cast since his injury during the dam collapse.

He had his hand on top of his graying head capping the loose hair that brushed his shoulders. She judged him to be in his midfifties because of the loose brown skin on his face and the deep crow's feet at his eyes. His lean frame bulged only slightly at the belly extending past his wide belt.

His brows rose at seeing her and he spoke into the phone. "I found her. Speak to you later." He hung up. "You want to tell me what you're doing up here, Detective?"

"You saw Wetselline's report?" she asked.

"Hell, yes, I did. You know what you're doing?"

"My sister is—"

He interrupted. "Sara Tah, mother of Louisa Tah, the last girl to go missing. It was in Wetselline's report. Funny that you never mentioned that in your interview."

She clamped her lips tight and waited.

Tinnin pressed his thumb and the knuckle of his index finger against the bridge of his nose and squeezed his eyes shut. He looked like he had a sinus infection but Ava suspected she was the cause of his headache.

"You up here doing your own investigation. Maybe bending a few rules. Is that it?"

She didn't deny it.

He dropped his hand away from his face. The chief rested both hands on his hips and lowered his chin. "Detective Hood, I know you are new here, but my law enforcement personnel follow procedure."

Ava waited for the other shoe to drop. It only took an eye-blink.

"You're off the case," he said.

"I'm not really on it yet. I'm on leave from my

office and I don't start here until next month. This is personal time."

"Detective, this is you coming up here to find the guilty. And the fact that you're not yet a member of my force, and might never be, doesn't keep you from following our laws."

"I'm here to find my niece."

"You could have been working on this case through proper channels," said Tinnin. "Instead of sneaking around up here doing who knows what. Why didn't you come to me?"

Ava lifted her chin. "I thought you might be involved."

He leaned back against the window sill behind him and folded his arms, glowering. "Cross me off your list, did you?"

She nodded.

"Why's that?"

"No motive. No opportunity and no evidence of any connection to my prime suspects."

"It's a small reservation, everyone is connected to everyone else somehow. Even you."

She'd do it all again. And the only way he was stopping her was to put her in his jail.

"I'm making progress."

"That so? By interfering with a murder investigation?"

"I found you Day's car and his body and I made certain that Redhorse didn't contaminate your crime scene." Now would be the time to mention Ty Red-horse. She didn't.

"I've got a call into your supervisor," said Tin-nin. "Let him know where you've been spending your vacation time."

The thing was she wasn't sorry. She knew the police were trying to recover the missing, but they were also investigating suspects to arrest and were slowed by making a case while she was unencumbered. If her actions meant that she got a reprimand, then so be it.

"And if you are doing anything illegal you need to stop."

She narrowed her eyes. "What would you do to get your son back?"

He leaned on his desk, hands flat so she could see both the red coral and the turquoise rings on the index and middle fingers of his right hand. They'd make really good brass knuckles, she thought.

"My older son is in the DEA somewhere in Oklahoma. Safe and sound, last I checked. My younger son is sixteen and sometimes I wish someone would take him."

"You don't mean that."

"No, I don't."

He straightened and waited.

"You can't have Hauser do the autopsy," she said.

He rolled his eyes. "I've got a ME in Darabee. He'll be lead. He's FBI but Hauser will think he's a sub. That all right with you, Hood? Or should I say Yokota?"

"I don't use that name."

"Yet it is the one that you used on the paperwork for your background check. Your legal name."

"Look, I'm not going to give you a whole family history, but my dad did not win father of the year. I don't know him. I don't use his name."

"Except when you have to."

"Exactly. If you've got the autopsy covered, then I'll leave you to your unpacking." Ava headed toward the door.

"Just a minute."

She turned to face him. He gave her a hard look.

"You take anything from my crime scene?"

"No, sir."

"Anything else you'd like me to know?"

"Redhorse asked me out."

Tinnin's hand dropped as he stared at her. "Jake?"

"Kee."

He looked to the ceiling of his office as if gathering his patience.

"Dr. Kee Redhorse, my suspect?"

"Yes, sir. Dinner tonight."

"Does he know who you are?"

"Yes."

Tinnin's shoulders relaxed.

"But not that I'm a detective. I also gave my name to Hector Hauser."

"Entrapment."

"No. I don't work for you. Anything I tell you would be from a witness. Anything I dig up is free information for you."

"You work for Saguaro. I've called your chief. He wants you home pronto."

She lowered her head, trying to avoid this. But she couldn't. So she drew back her shoulders. Then she said, "I'll resign."

"You break the law and I'll arrest you."

"No, Chief. You'll thank me because I'm going to bring you the person or persons who did this."

"Going to solve the whole thing all by your lonesome. Is that it?"

Ava pulled a face but did not reply as she withdrew a folded page from her pocket and set it on the worn surface of his battered wooden desk.

"What's this?"

"Dr. Hauser is having instant message sex with his receptionist."

He regarded the paper.

"How did you get this?"

She met his gaze and did not answer.

"How, Ava?"

"Any evidence that comes into your possession is admissible as long as you didn't break the law to get it. So…"

"You're going to lose everything," he warned.

"As long as I get her back."

"Not necessarily going to work out like that. Kacey Doka nearly got herself killed trying a similar stunt when she showed up unprotected at the clinic and nearly ended up recaptured."

"I read that because of her actions, they found two-dozen girls in a camp out in the desert north of my reservation."

"Twenty-three women," he said.

"Sounds to me like she made the right choice."

"We follow the law here and you swore an oath."

She nodded her head. "Protect and serve. That's what I'm doing, Chief."

"What if they go after your sister or her kids?"

Ava stilled. She'd thought of that, of course, and it chilled her blood. It was one thing to endanger her own life, but not those three little girls or her sister. But if she gave up now, Louisa would never come home. She knew it in her heart.

"A tough choice," said Tinnin.

Ava pressed her teeth together, not trusting her voice.

Tinnin frowned and then rested a hand on his hip, regarding her for a long moment.

"There were no prints on the bike," he said.

She could not hide her surprise on that one. "Day's bike?"

He nodded.

"You mean other than Day's?" she asked.

"No. Not even Day's. Wiped clean."

Her heart accelerated at the implication.

"You listing this as homicide?" she asked.

"Open case," he said. "But I've got questions."

"I noticed something odd on your tribe's website." She motioned to his laptop. "May I?"

He turned it toward her and she sat before his desk, opened a browser and loaded the tribe's website. As it loaded she wondered absently how many years it took to wear the varnish off the surface.

When the site appeared she logged in.

"You have to be a member to access this part of the site," he said.

"My sister was checking," said Ava and glanced up to see his sour expression. Then she pointed at the spreadsheet.

He rounded the desk to look at the screen, limping as he advanced.

"Looks like no casino profits are needed for the clinic's operation."

He squinted at the screen and then looked to her.

"Most people don't really look at what's not listed on a budget. But I'm wondering where you get your clinic's operations budget. The equipment in the clinic? Radiology area, women's health clinic, three exam rooms and a fully stocked procedure room on-site."

"I think they operate on grant money and Medicare. State of Arizona chips in, too," said Tinnin, hand now working the muscles at the back of his neck.

Ava shook her head. "Our health clinic takes twenty-two percent of our entire operating budget from the casino profits, in addition to Medicare, and yours runs itself." She smiled. "Lucky you."

Tinnin sat on the edge of the desk and folded his hands on one thigh. "You have my attention."

Chapter Eight

"Your clinic includes…" Ava leaned in and clicked to another screen that showed Dr. Hauser's photo in an article on the tribe's website. Ava placed her finger on the line of text and read to Chief Tinnin from the page, "'a full-service, highly complex laboratory working with state-of-the-art diagnostic equipment providing a spectrum of tests necessary to diagnose and treat many medical problems.' Yada, yada… 'drawing blood and…staffed with trained lab personnel.'" She turned to him. "You have only three doctors but you have a full-service lab? Meanwhile, our blood and samples go out daily to a lab for testing. I checked."

Tinnin shrugged.

"Lab like that could run pregnancy tests in-house. Pretty fast, too, I'll bet," said Ava, thinking of the baby ring.

"So who's on your short list?"

"Dr. Redhorse and Dr. Hauser and Ms. Betty Mills. Any of the nurses might be involved along with the lab techs."

"Not Lori Mott. She was the one who discovered the girls had all been seen there shortly before their disappearances."

"And she's married to Kee's brother Jake," said Ava. "One of our officers."

"Gives her insider info on your investigation."

"No way."

Ava shrugged. "Maybe not. Turning them in doesn't make sense if she's involved, of course."

"We are looking at Kee and Hector very seriously," said Tinnin.

"So if you know Hauser might be involved, why let him do the autopsy on Day?"

Tinnin grinned and scratched beneath his chin.

"Unless…you wanted to use it as bait."

"If he tries to access that body early, I will know. If he meddles with the evidence, I'll know. We already took samples."

"His nails?"

"You noticed that in the dark?"

She nodded.

"Yeah, we have skin samples. Should have something in a few days."

"So we're good?" said Ava.

"Not exactly." He stood. "I spoke to your captain. I've told him that we are withdrawing our offer for employment. He wants you back home tomorrow."

KEE COVERED THE urgent care clinic solo most of Wednesday morning so Dr. Hauser could perform the autopsy on Day. Kee didn't envy him that. Being the ME for their tribe put Hector in the center of much human tragedy. He saw the worst of them, no question.

They were full up since the clinic was closing

at noon instead of four so they could move back to Piñon Flats. Betty told him that Dr. Hauser was en route back from the autopsy and would meet them at the clinic. Dr. Hauser had held the position as ME since before Kee was even born. If he did retire, would that be Kee's duty, as well?

He finished the last of the patients at one o'clock, instead of noon. Betty brought him a sandwich to munch as he boxed his personal gear and afterward helped see their equipment into a tractor trailer. Much of their supplies had remained in Piñon Flats and he would be so happy to be back where they had better facilities and more room. The tribe was recovering from the crisis.

When Kee arrived, Betty Mills was already at her post at reception working on a backlog of paperwork.

Hauser was there behind the desk as Kee arrived carrying a box.

Hauser spotted Kee and smiled broadly. "Welcome home!"

Kee returned the smile. "Thanks. It's good to be back."

He didn't say great because Dr. Day was not here. And it didn't feel the same here since the eco-extremists attack that had changed their river forever and now the death of a colleague. Perhaps it was the beginning of a new normal and the worst was behind them. He hoped so, at least.

"How did it go this morning?" Kee asked.

"Nothing unexpected. Bruises I saw were consistent with the fall and his neck was broken. Likely died instantly."

Instantly, after falling all the way to the ground, thought Kee. What must he have been thinking as he careened through space? Kee shuddered.

"Cold?" said Hauser. "What's the A/C set at, Betty?"

"Seventy-five, as always."

"Well, you're just in from the heat. You'll adjust." Hauser gave him a friendly pat on the shoulder.

"So you don't think he fell?" asked Kee.

"Yes. Manner of death was a fall. Cause of death, accidental. My report will say as much."

Kee shifted a moving box to his hip.

"Well, get your office set up. We open tomorrow."

They spent the afternoon settling in but did open for a tribe member who was in active labor. His sister-in-law Lori did all the heavy lifting since she had more experience with delivery than he did. But he assisted and when he checked the wall clock for a time of birth, he realized he'd been working for ten hours straight and that if he was going to pick Ava up for a dinner date, he needed to get out of here.

"I have to go," he said to Lori.

"Hot date?" joked Lori.

"I sure hope so."

Her brows lifted and then she laughed. "Well, good for you. Hell, yeah, and about time. Anyone I know?"

"She's the sister of Sara Tah," said Kee.

Lori's smile wavered at this. No one who heard Sara's name was not reminded of her husband's recent and very untimely death and the daughter who had gone missing at the beginning of the month.

"I know," he said. "She's here to help out. And she's terrific."

"Sara is from Saguaro Flats. Right?"

"Yes."

"So what's her sister do down there among the cactus, swimming pools and Anglos?"

"I'm trying to figure that out."

"Well, have fun."

He made it back to Turquoise Ridge at seven thirty. He called Ava's phone but got no answer. He showered and dressed and called again at eight with the sinking feeling that he was too late for supper.

There was a knock on the trailer door as he was sliding his phone into his front pocket. His dress shirt was open showing a wide swath of medium brown skin and his hair was sticking up with the product he'd tried and not yet tamed.

The knock came again and he jogged the rest of the way, fastening his belt buckle just before he reached the door and pulled it open.

There stood Ava, dressed in an oversize sweater with a scoop neck that showed smooth tawny skin flushed with a rosy color and draped with a thin gold chain that caught the light. Kee felt his pulse beating in his veins as he lifted his gaze to meet hers.

"I'm so sorry I'm so late. I tried to call."

"I know. I was driving. I called the clinic and spoke to your sister-in-law. She said you just delivered a bouncing baby boy." Ava's generous smile made his body tingle.

"Yes. Well, she and the mother did most of it."

She held out a large brown paper bag and a bottle of ice tea to him. He took the bags and she hiked up the strap to her oversize purse.

"What's this?" he asked regarding the bag.

"Picnic supper. I have potato salad, fry bread, pulled pork, corn and chocolate cream pie."

"Oh, but I wanted to take you out," he said.

"You had a hard day." They were all hard, which was why he slept so well.

"And...this is more private," she said.

He lifted his brows at the implication and she gave him a coy smile. Despite his disappointment at not being about to take her out, his body reacted instantly to her suggestion of privacy. He'd like to have some private time with Ava, after he figured out what was going on.

Her kiss and Ty's discovery that Ava carried a concealed weapon had kept him up last night and the more he thought about it the more he wondered who she was and what she was up to. He didn't know but he planned to find out. And when he did, after he did, perhaps he wouldn't be so enamored. Ava was just too good to be true. He knew it.

"Unless you want to get out of this trailer?" she asked after his hesitance.

He stepped aside and motioned her in.

"No, this is fine. Let me set the table."

She stepped past him. "Mind if I use the bathroom? Too much coffee today."

"Sure." He took the bags and went with them to the kitchen. She followed as far as the dinette, where she draped her purse over a chair back. Then she did go into the bathroom, but upon exiting she crossed to Day's bedroom. His eyes narrowed.

He unpacked their dinner. By the time she got back he had his shirt buttoned, the table set and was working on pouring drinks. She glanced at her bag and then to him. There was something off about her. And what was she doing in Richard's bedroom?

"Are you sure this is all right?" he said.

"Why? Because I brought you a meal?"

"That's part of it." Come to think of it, not one woman in his experience had ever reached in her pocket to pay for anything.

"Kee, I went to community college but I worked my way through. I can only imagine what it cost to go to medical school. You don't need to impress me with a fancy meal."

That was a switch. The women he'd met did not understand that residents worked long hours for not very much money. They heard doctor and made assumptions. Had he finally found a girl who was not drawn to the lure of prestige and money?

Or did she want something else?

She was drawn to something. But he wasn't entirely sure what that something was.

"Well, I owe you a meal," he said.

"If you cook it, I'll eat it," she promised.

"Oh, well, I'm not much of a cook."

"You survived medical school—you must know how to make something."

He laughed. "Spaghetti and meat sauce, Cup O' Noodles, mac and cheese, brownies from a box."

"That's nearly a complete meal."

"Steamed broccoli."

"There you go!"

He laughed.

"Spaghetti is my favorite." She wiggled her eyebrows. "Grilled cheese is second and I love a burger made any way out of anything as long as it had four hooves."

"Refined taste."

"Hey, I ponied up for the ice tea, didn't I?"

They were both laughing now. He liked her, damn it. But he didn't like being tricked or used. Ava wasn't here for dinner. He knew that much.

His smile faded.

"What's wrong?"

"Oh, sorry. I was just thinking how much I am enjoying myself and how much I like you and then I thought of Richard. It's just terrible."

She nodded and laid a hand on his shoulder, rubbing up and down. "I'm sorry this happened. Did Dr. Hauser say what caused Dr. Day's death?"

"Accident, he said."

Ava's eyes narrowed but she said nothing to this.

He turned toward her and took her hand. He tugged to draw her closer but she resisted so he leaned forward and dropped a soft, gentle kiss on her mouth.

It might have been perfect if not for his reservations. She was up to something. But what?

He drew back.

She rounded the table. Kee glanced at her purse hanging from the chair back. It gaped open. Inside he saw a black pistol in a stitched leather holster with a quick draw feature. Clipped to the holster was a gold badge that read *Saguaro Flats Tribal Police Detective*.

He lifted the weapon and badge and held them in two hands. So, Ty had been right all along.

Chapter Nine

Ava held her second pistol in her hand, straight down at her side away from Kee's line of sight. He'd found her empty pistol and badge, both of which he held in his open hands with a look of utter confusion on his face. His mouth gaped and his brow wrinkled. A quicksilver flash of panic washed over her as she realized this was it, the test she hoped he'd pass.

Finally!

Had he handled enough weapons to know what one felt like with an empty clip? She knew he hadn't touched her purse before because it was exactly as she had left it, right down to the twisted strap and zipper not quite done up. That made her resort to leaving it unzipped and hanging half-open.

She met his accusatory stare and waited for what he would do next. His mouth turned down in a tight angry frown and the muscles at his jaw bulged.

She pressed her arms tight to her sides, feeling the Kevlar vest beneath her bulky sweater and the weight of the pistol gripped tight in her hand. Her mouth was dry and her heartbeat raced as she waited for him to reveal himself.

He dropped the holstered weapon and badge to the kitchen table. It thumped to the surface, making the silverware clatter.

"A badge," he said, leveling her with a hard look. "Makes sense."

"Yes," she admitted, as her heart continued to prepare her for whatever came next. But she could breathe now. She relaxed her hand, flicking the safety back on as she kept her eyes trained on Kee. Was he this cool a customer or was he innocent? Every day this took was another day Louisa was trapped in some horrible place. She just had to get her home.

She knew confronting Kee like this was in direct conflict with what the Turquoise Canyon police force wanted her to do. But they knew why she was here and every day that her niece was being held captive against her will was torture. She wasn't going to wait around and play nice.

"Officer. It's what Ty called you. He knew."

She remembered, of course.

"What kind of game are you playing, Detective?"

She lifted one hand in a gesture meant for him to halt as she crept forward. "Step away from the table, Kee."

He did, complying exactly with her order. But he did not look frightened or surprised. He just looked defeated as he stomped to the window and lifted his hands.

"I should have known that you were after something, too. Just not me."

She wished it could be different. Wished she could be the woman he believed her to be. But she had tricked him and that would not be easily forgotten. He was allowed to be angry.

She retrieved her weapon, holster and badge, returning them to the bag and setting them on the chair before her.

"You want to frisk me or maybe kiss me again? How about I wait here while you finish searching Richard's room?"

Ava crept forward, returned the clip to the pistol and holstered her weapon at her hip. Then she slipped the second firearm into her purse. Finally, she pressed her palm to the table as she released a long breath.

"You think I was going to shoot you, Ava? I've spent too many hours stitching up bodies to do that."

"I'm sorry. I had to find out what you would do."

"This was a test? I don't know who or what you think I am, but I think I deserve an explanation."

"I'm here to find my niece."

He folded his arms but did not look the least bit guilty or surprised. "Okay. I don't know what that has to do with me, so keep going."

"Why don't you sit down," she said.

"I'll stay right here, thanks."

She had thought about this at length and had still not decided how much to tell him. Kee had known her name for four days. That was more than enough to figure out who she was and make a move. He hadn't. Yesterday, she'd given her name to Hauser. If he and Hauser were involved with the disappearances, less information was better. If Hauser was working without Kee, then Kee could be an asset. Plus, if he was not involved, he deserved to know.

"Why are you looking for your niece in Richard's room?"

She forced her arms down away from her service pistol and sat herself backward in a kitchen chair. Kee leaned against the counter beside the window across from her, arms now tightly folded in a defensive posture that echoed the tight lines in his handsome face.

"One of the nurses on your staff discovered something in your clinic's medical records. She brought it to your tribal police. Kee, all the missing girls were seen at your clinic."

He blinked at this revelation and then scowled. "Of course they all were. Almost every single member of this tribe has been treated there. You might as well check the tribal registration records. The names are all there, as well."

"No, Kee, it's worse than that." She swallowed and rested both forearms on the chair back. "The girls all attended different schools, from Turquoise Ridge to Koun'nde to Piñon Flats. They didn't all know each other, but they were all treated at the tribe's women's health clinic at least twice over the course of a single month each and disappeared within days of their second visit."

His shoulders relaxed as the angry expression eased to be replaced by worry.

"That's odd."

He didn't ask which nurse, she realized. A guilty man would likely want to know who had leaked information to the police.

"I've spoken to Zella Colelay. You know her?"

"Yes."

"Have you treated her?"

"No. I don't think so."

"Within the last year?"

"What was her condition?"

"She had an infection."

"I didn't treat her."

The medical records said that he did. Lori had given them to tribal police and Ava had spoken at length to Lori Redhorse. But Ava didn't have those records. Not yet.

She couldn't wait to join the Turquoise Canyon police force to get them. That only left Kee.

"Zella was warned by Marta Garcia that someone was following her. When Marta went missing, Zella dropped out of school, hid and escaped capture."

"Did you say capture?"

"Yes."

"I thought these girls were runaways."

"Zella didn't run. She delivered a baby that your brother Jake adopted. You must know that."

"I've seen Jake and Lori and their baby, Fortune. I didn't know Zella was the birth mother. That seems odd because…"

She finished his sentence. "Because Fortune is white."

Kee nodded. "She seems to be, at least. Jake found her in his truck."

"Yes, I know," said Ava.

"How many girls are missing?"

"Five. That does not include Kacey."

"That's related? Kacey coming back? Her coming home pregnant?"

"How do you know about that?" she asked.

"Colt called me. He was with my brother Jake and having some psychological problems. He's got PTSD since his service in Afghanistan. I got a therapist here to see him, outside actually, because he wouldn't come in the clinic. He wanted to know if Kacey was all right. He said she was in labor and in Darabee Hospital. I checked that information for him and she was there. Delivered a baby girl."

"Where is Colt now?"

"I don't know. Last Tuesday, he was at Darabee Hospital. But he checked himself out. I've been to his cabin. But he only lets Ty see him."

Ava's shoulders tightened. A week ago Ty and Colt might well have been talking. But not anymore. Clearly, Kee did not know that Colt and Kacey had left the rez with the Justice Department or that Ty was under investigation.

"Did you check with Ty?"

"Of course. He says Colt and Kacey are off on some road trip."

"Is that right?" It wasn't.

"I doubt it. Ty often covers for Colt. Besides, who takes a baby on a road trip? My mother seems to know something but she won't say, either. Just said that he'll be gone for a while. Does this have to do with…"

"He's in witness protection. He and Kacey both. That's what Lori told me."

Kee's mouth dropped open. A hand went to his forehead.

"Why didn't Jake tell me?"

"Because he's a law enforcement officer and would be breaking federal law by revealing your brother's status."

"By telling me? I'm his brother." His voice held a sharp edge she had not heard before.

"You are a suspect."

"Wait a second. Where are you getting this? Why not go to the police here?"

"I theorized that someone in the force could be involved in the disappearances."

His brows lifted. "Your badge says Saguaro Flats."

"That's right."

"So you have no authority here."

"Also right."

His eyes narrowed on her. "So how did you get all this information?"

"First from my department. Your chief gave us a courtesy call. When Louisa went missing, I came up here and interviewed with your tribal police. When I was hired, I was briefed in preparation for my appointment as a new detective here. That probably won't happen now."

"Does Ty know who you are?"

"He suspects. Also, you should know that he's under federal investigation for his part in transporting Kacey Doka back into the hands of her captors."

"What?"

"All related." She tried and failed to remain unaffected by the grief now clearly evident in Kee's expression.

Kee reached for the closest chair and sat hard.

"I checked your personal computer. Day wasn't a suspect, so I had no need to check his but after his death, I thought I had better have a look."

"But the police already took it."

"Exactly."

"So you show up here bearing take-out dinner and make me think you want some alone time, just so you can search my place."

"I did that over a week ago. Tonight was just to see your reaction."

"That's just great."

She shrugged. "She's my niece."

A suspect's first reaction would not be self-righteousness, she thought. Ava's chest ached in something that she thought might be sympathy for his hurt and confusion. This was new ground and she did not like the feelings he stirred in her.

"Does your job as a police officer give you permission to hack my computer?"

"No." He had her if he wanted her. He could just pick up the phone and call his tribal police. She waited as their eyes met.

"So you've gone off the reservation, literally. I'm not a cop, but I know you can't obtain evidence like this. You can't break in without permission from our tribal leadership or without a warrant from the police."

She laid it out there, trying to make him understand.

"I'm not trying to build a case here, Kee. I'm trying to find my niece before she disappears forever. What do you think happens to those girls after they give birth?"

He ground his teeth. Her heart hammered as she waited for him to decide.

"I could pick up the phone and call the real police and have you arrested. Right?"

She nodded. "That's correct. You could also press charges."

He rubbed his hand over his broad forehead as if trying to come up with the right move. He held her freedom in the balance.

He dropped his hand and faced her across the table, his face pale and grave. "Give me a reason not to call Chief Tinnin."

"Because then you might never know who did this."

Kee slapped a hand on the table, making the silverware shake. "You're wrong, you know."

"About?"

"About me and about my clinic. We are helping people. I am never alone with a female patient. It's for my protection as much as theirs. We have procedures that are followed to the letter. We sure as hell don't kidnap them or inseminate them. We're doctors."

She held her tongue.

"It's not Hector," said Kee.

"If you'd like to prove that, you're going to need to help me."

"Help you how?"

"Get me those records."

"No."

"I've ruled you out. Hauser is now my focus."

He made a sound of disbelief choked in a laugh. "Hector? He's the founder of our clinic."

"He also may have arranged for six women to be kidnapped."

"I'm not going to betray my friends," said Kee.

"Even if they are feeding your children to these criminals?"

"That could be anyone on the reservation."

"I know each missing girl was seen by your clinic shortly before their disappearances. I know that your name is on the record as treating each one of those girls."

Kee gasped. "That's impossible."

"Not according to my sources."

"I never treated any of them!"

"Either you did or someone from *your* clinic changed the records."

"You have these records?"

"Not yet."

"But you've seen them?"

"I've heard from a credible source."

"Hearsay, you mean. You have nothing. No proof."

"I have a dead body."

"Day's death is unrelated to what you are alleging."

She made a sound deep in the back of her throat.

Kee continued on. "We would never, ever do something like this."

"You sure about that?"

"Absolutely."

"Willing to put your money where your mouth is?"

"What does that mean?" he asked.

"Well, if everything is hunky-dory at your clinic, then you won't mind checking the girls' records. I'll give you the names and you see who treated them and if it's you, we talk some more."

He considered the proposal and then dipped his chin. "All right."

Chapter Ten

"I can't believe I agreed to this. There could be serious consequences for breaking patients' rights."

She cocked her head to stare at him. "That's your concern? Breaking the rules? We are talking about young girls captured and taken."

Kee turned his troubled eyes on her. "Ava, what you say is happening is truly heinous, but my clinic had nothing to do with it. This is the first time I've heard that the disappearances might be tied to our clinic."

Ava shook her head. "If not you, then it's Hauser."

"No. No way. Hector is one of the best men I know. Right down deep inside. He's a good doctor and a loving husband. He's raised a son who is a credit to this tribe."

She folded her arms. "People are not always what they seem. And as for the records, I'll bet you that your name appears on every damn one," she said.

"That's impossible. I rarely work in the women's health clinic."

"That's Hector's baby, so to speak," Ava provided.

"Yes."

She lifted her brows. She was certain that Hector was involved. She just wasn't sure about Kee.

"So what will you do if your name is listed as

the treating physician for all appointments for the missing girls?" she asked.

"That won't happen," he said, a determined set to his jaw.

"Humor me."

"If so, well, I'd go to Hector."

"Nope. Wrong answer. Someone pushed Richard off a cliff."

"Not Hector."

"He's dirty." She made a face and waited.

"No. He's our ME. He's…"

"I'll bet that someone thought Day knew something. And I'll also bet that someone is Hector. So you do not want to let him know you think he might be tied up in this."

"I don't. He's not," Kee said, shaking his head in denial, but his eyes looked wide and worried.

"We saw Day's body, Kee. You saw blood and tissue under his fingernails. The kind of thing you see when someone is fighting for their life."

"It's up to the medical examiner to determine if that blood was Day's." Kee's heart sank. Hector was the ME. The hopelessness grew inside him like a parasite.

She didn't let up. "How did Hauser feel about Dr. Day?"

Kee looked away and she had her answer before he spoke.

"He didn't trust him." Kee shrugged. "An outsider."

"Kee, look at me."

Dark troubled eyes met hers and he held himself across the middle as if in physical pain. It was a posture she recognized from the times she had to give family members bad news. Hector was important to Kee. Not just a boss, but a role model, and he was so far up on a pedestal that the fall would be spectacular.

"This is no coincidence. It's not someone else. It's you or Hector or it's you *and* Hector."

"I had your gun. If it were me..."

"Yes, you passed that test. It's why we are having this conversation. My gut tells me that you're a good guy, Kee, if a little too trusting of those you love. Plus I took precautions." She lifted her bulky sweater and showed him her body armor and the pistol holstered at her hip. "This one was empty. I have another in there," she said, motioning to her bag.

"You thought I'd shoot you!" He lifted to his feet and threw his hands in the air. His face felt hot and his fingers tingled. He could not remember ever being this angry. His indignation beat inside him with his pounding heart.

She lifted her chin and set her jaw, waiting.

His voice emerged between clenched teeth. "I don't like being used."

She held her ground against his indignation. "It's a homicide investigation that includes six kidnappings."

He was shaking his head in a slow, steady beat, as if he'd stopped listening. Then he turned away and began pacing back and forth across the narrow kitchen like a criminal in lockup. "Jake's been avoiding me. I've left messages. He wasn't allowed to talk to me. Is that right?"

"I'm sure he was warned not to do so."

"Ty?"

"He's up to his neck. His involvement is contradictory. But I know he is under investigation."

Ava was very confused by Ty Redhorse's behavior. It almost seemed as if he wanted to appear to be in the gang but help the police. It seemed that he had picked his brothers over the gang on at least two occasions.

Kee rose from the chair, stumbled the three steps to the couch and fell back into the cushions. Ava tracked him, her hand going to the warm, familiar grip of her gun. He sat and Ava waited.

"This can't be happening," said Kee.

She almost felt sorry for him. Then she recalled what Lori had told her of Kacey's captivity, months in a basement with a mattress on the floor. Kacey had escaped while in active labor and she'd been very lucky to make it to her rez and to a man capable of defending her. Whatever Colt's mental health issues, he was a protector. Kacey's decision to try to lure the Russians into recapturing her had not led to finding her friends, as she had hoped. But it did lead to the FBI finding another group of imprisoned women. Unfortunately, her decision to leave protection also drew Ty into the middle of a bad situation. Ava suspected that the tribe's gang had sent Ty to recover her because as her boyfriend's brother, Kacey might trust him. What she had not figured out was if Ty was working with the gang to recapture Kacey or with Colt to recover her.

Kee sat with his head in his hands and Ava resisted the urge to go and sit beside him. Comfort him. The urge was so overwhelming she had to fold her arms over her chest and move in the opposite direction. That brought her to the short kitchen counter adjacent to the couch.

At last he lifted his head. His eyes were now bloodshot and he seemed like a man who had just received word of a death in the family. Grief deepened the lines about his mouth and gave his eyes a lost quality.

"Kee?"

"I don't believe this. I don't believe you. Hector is a good man."

"Perhaps in some ways."

"You said it is him or me. I know it's not me. So you want me to believe that the man who changed my life, gave me two straight legs, encouraged me, pushed me and helped me to become a physician— you want me to believe that that man is capable of... of this?" He pinched his eyes shut and gripped the bridge of his nose with a thumb and forefinger.

Ava struggled not to go to him, comfort him. Instead she focused on controlling the tightness in her chest as it moved to her stomach. "Yes."

She lifted her hand to him but he stepped out of her reach. She let her hand drop back to her side. He had every right to be angry and upset. She'd just kicked a hole in his perceptions. It would take time to come to grips with everything she had hit him with. She wondered if he would ever forgive her.

"But why? Why would anyone do such a thing?"

She blew away a breath but failed to control the internal turmoil caused by his upset. "Most crimes fall into three categories: rage, revenge or money."

"He doesn't have a lot of money," Kee argued.

"He has a clinic."

Kee sat back, confusion now furrowing his brow. "What?"

"You said he built it from the ground up. You said you have a facility to rival any like it. How did that happen without money?"

"The tribe…the casino…" He shook his head, bewildered.

"Nope. Tribal budget lists zero operating budget for your clinic. Operational budget comes from federal subsidies and grants."

"That's impossible," he whispered.

"Exactly."

He stared at her as if seeing her for the first time. His arms lay limp at his sides as if all the life had drained out of him. Would he give up or fight?

"You could help me, Kee. You're a good guy.

I know you want the truth. You could help us get those girls back home to their families."

"Which girls do you suspect have been taken? Tell me the girl's names."

She listed them in order of disappearance. "Elsie Weaver, November; Marta Garcia, February; Kacey Doka, February; Brenda Espinoza, May; Maggie Kesselman, September; and my niece, Louisa Tah, October second. She's sixteen by the way."

His head sunk. "I know their families. They don't miss them."

"What's that supposed to mean?" she asked.

He gave her a hard stare. "Let's take your sister, Sara. She didn't file a missing person's report. The school did. Noted that Louisa was absent and checked her home. She'd been missing for days."

Now it was Ava's jaw swung open and she staggered back. Her hands clamped over her heart, which squeezed painfully. Her throat burned and she feared for a moment she would cry. Somehow she forced her words past her constricted throat. "How many days?"

"I don't know. Three. Four. The point is, how do you not notice your daughter not coming home?"

Ava had no answer. She felt her insides churn with outrage and disbelief. How could Sara have ignored her own daughter's welfare? She tried to think past the pain. "Maybe that is how they were chosen. Hector picked girls from troubled families."

Kee rose to his feet. "Stop talking about him as if he's guilty."

So, he was going to fight. Fight for the man he trusted and loved. She could work with that.

"Are you a detective at Saguaro Flats?"

"Suspended," she said.

"Because of this?"

She gave a slow nod.

He looked to someplace beyond her, his gaze going out of focus. "My mom is fostering the Doka girls."

She knew that and thought it was both the kind and right thing to do.

"Those are Kacey's sisters."

"That's another thing. Those girls are your family now because Kacey and Colt are married."

He cradled his chin in his palm and braced his elbow in the cup of his other hand. He looked as if he had a toothache instead of a heartache. If he was innocent, she had just dropped another bomb in the epicenter of his world.

His eyes were watery as he stared at the floor. He did not look like a man caught in a web of lies. He looked like one who had just found that his foundation was made of sand.

He lifted his gaze to meet hers. His fingers brushed over his lips and settled on the opposite side, the pads curling under his jaw.

"All this, Colt, Day's death, Ty's involvement, even the clinic connection with the missing women, all this has been going on right under my nose because I've been too damn buried in work to notice. That's what you are saying."

"I'm sorry, Kee." She stood and came to perch on the arm of the couch opposite him. "Sometimes it's hardest to see what is right in front of you."

His hand dropped, folding protectively over his chest. "I've been killing myself at the clinic. Killing myself to pay the bills. Until yesterday, I was beating myself up because I thought I had to leave here in order to stay afloat, and then a miracle happened that enabled me to stay, to make a difference. I've been so busy burning the candle at both ends trying to make good that I haven't given the missing girls the attention they deserved. Hell, I don't even know what's going on with my own family." He blew out a breath, his frustration evident. "I thought I was a part of something great. You're telling me it's all twisted. Rotten."

"It appears so to me."

"Then I want to know what is happening. What is really happening. Not your theory or whatever. I want solid proof that what you theorize is true."

"I can work with that. Shall we go have a look at Day's room together?"

Chapter Eleven

Ava drove the short distance from Kee's trailer to her sister's. The first thing she noticed was that the lights were out and Sara's car was gone. Had something happened to them?

Ava threw open the door as panic washed through her, and she ran to the door, finding it unlocked. A quick check inside showed that all three girls were asleep in their beds but their mother was not in the trailer. Ava stormed back to the kitchen and caught the glint of an empty liquor bottle on the counter and another in the trash. She reached the kitchen sink and gripped the bottle as the rage thundered inside her.

Had Sara seriously left these girls alone here?

She was reaching for her phone when headlights flashed around the room and then went out. Ava watched Sara exit the car, holding a bag in one hand as she walked toward the entrance. She touched the hood of the car three times on her slow journey. A moment later the doorknob turned ever so slowly. Ava waited. When Sara was halfway to the kitchen, Ava flicked on the light. Sara gasped and jumped. Then she clutched the brown bag to her chest. Ava recognized the size and shape. It was a liquor bottle. The extra large sort, and Sara clutched the neck in one fist and cradled the bottom in the other.

"Ava. What are you doing here?"

Was she serious? Hadn't Sara even seen her car?

"I thought you were on a date."

"You left them alone," said Ava, her voice a growl.

Sara waved a dismissive hand and chuckled. "Just for a few minutes. They're fine."

"Is Louisa fine?"

Sara's smile dropped. She teetered and then side-stepped before regaining her balance.

"What do you mean?" said Sara, still clutching her bottle.

"You didn't even know she was missing."

"Yes, I did."

"When did you see her last?"

"Sunday, I think. Day before the school called."

"And she was out all night?"

Sara's chin fell. The arm holding the liquor dropped to her side as she pressed her opposite hand to her forehead.

"Maybe it was Saturday I saw her."

Ava rocked back against the counter. "Which was it?"

Sara lifted her eyes to meet Ava's and those eyes were bloodshot and filling with tears.

Her words were a wail. "I don't know."

Ava almost went to her. Almost took her in her arms. She took a step in that direction and then she stopped, spun and threw the empty bottle she held into the trash on top of the other with enough force to shatter both. Then she rounded on Sara. "Give me that bottle."

Sara did. Ava dumped the contents down the drain.

GOING TO WORK on Thursday was harder than taking the medical boards. How did one act around a mentor that had overnight become a stranger? Kee's main tactic was avoidance.

Something bad was happening here. Last night they'd discovered a file with print copies of emails Richard had written to his FEMA supervisors regarding Dr. Hauser's refusal to allow him to input his medical data or allow him access to the clinic's records. That in itself was exceedingly odd. But it got worse.

Ava had been right. Kee was listed as the attending physician for each of the missing girls' visits and "his" notes on each visit were included. They looked for all the world as if he had written them. But he knew he had not.

It was as if he had woken up this morning in a parallel universe where everything looked the same but was badly and dangerously different. There was physical pain at learning that the man he so respected and admired had used him. Betrayal mixed with a sense of his own failures to make it hard to think.

Somehow he struggled through the day and left the clinic early that evening. Mills and Hauser were still there and waved him out, promising to lock up. Why did their smiles no longer seem to meet their eyes?

Kee drove to his mother's place for dinner. Housing was tight now in Piñon Flats as the tribe returned to their homes and the FEMA trailers were being reclaimed. His trailer was scheduled for pickup tomorrow, so he had been there to remove his gear. Richard's personal belongings had already been boxed and shipped to his family. Kee supposed he could sleep there tonight but now that he suspected Richard had been murdered, he just didn't feel comfortable there. Instead, he'd be sleeping on his mother's couch until he could make other arrangements.

He needed his own place because of the Doka girls now fostered at his childhood home. Two of them were staying in the room that had once belonged to Colt and Jake. The other girl was sharing his sister Abbie's room.

Where was Ava tonight? Was she working on the Day case or something else? Ava was the first woman he'd taken notice of in years. He didn't know what made him feel more furious, that she'd used him or the recognition that, even knowing what she had done, he still cared what she was doing. He reached for the door, which was never locked, and paused as he noticed his hand was shaking. He squeezed his fingers into a fist and swallowed down the lump in his throat. After several deep breaths, the tightness in his chest eased and he let himself into his mom's entryway.

Ava had used him. Still, he would hand over the medical records that could get him fired or possibly cost him his license to practice medicine.

His mother knew something was wrong with him at first glance. She was perceptive that way. After the girls were all in their rooms for the night, he sat with her at her kitchen table, automatically taking the seat he had used during his growing-up years.

"I heard about Dr. Day," she said, guessing at the reason he was upset and guessing correctly, in part.

"Yes, it's a blow." He looked at his mother and wondered if he knew her at all. "You didn't tell me about Colt being in witness protection."

Her inhalation was sharp. "Did Ty tell you?"

Kee shook his head. "Can't say where I heard."

"I was going to tell you, Kee. Despite what Ty told me."

"What did he say?"

"Not too much. That you could get in trouble or worse, get hurt. But I was going to tell you. It all happened so fast and you haven't been around much since the dam break."

"You could call me, Mom."

She shook her head. "Not the kind of thing I can say on the phone."

"All right. So where's Colt?"

His mom leaned in and lowered her voice to a whisper. "We're not supposed to know. It's witness protection and they just up and take them someplace where they don't know a soul and we can't contact him and he can't call or write. It's how they keep them safe. But Ty followed him. He's always looked out for his baby brother and I feel better knowing."

"Where?"

"Kenai, Alaska. Colt is some kind of commercial fisherman."

"And he's married?"

"Yes. I was at the wedding and so was Ty. The ceremony was at the compound just last week. Don't feel bad. Jake missed it, too."

"But he at least knew about it."

His mother pressed her hands flat on her worn tabletop. "Jake explained everything to me. He said you couldn't be seen there because you were undercover at the clinic."

Kee's brows lifted. *Undercover?* Was that Jake's way of protecting their mom from the truth that he was a suspect in a surrogate baby ring?

"He told you that?" Kee told his mom about Ava and how she had hacked his computer, broken at least a dozen laws and found Richard's body.

"You could have her arrested."

"Seems that way."

"So why don't you turn her in?"

He leaned forward, resting his elbows on his knees and lacing his fingers together. "Because I think she may be right that the disappearances of our girls is somehow connected to our clinic."

"That can't be. Can it?" asked his mother.

Kee cleared his throat. "I don't even know anymore."

"All you kids were treated by Dr. Hauser. I trusted him with each one of you. He treated every illness and stitched you all up more than once. And your legs, well, I can't ever repay him for that. How could he do something like this?"

Kee had no answer.

His mother gasped. "He just gave Abbie her sports physical for volleyball."

Kee felt an instant surge of fury. His pulse pounded in his ears and he clenched his fists. If Dr. Hauser had harmed his sister…

"Maybe your cop lady's just wrong about everything," said his mom.

"I hope so. But I know that Lori thinks so and Ava is certain. She doesn't have the proof yet."

"Our Lori?" asked his mother.

"Yes. Jake's Lori. She found something. Now I've seen it, too. All the girls were seen at our clinic only days before they vanished."

"A coincidence?" asked his mother, but her expression had changed from disbelief to one of worry.

"I sure hope so."

The silence was broken only by the occasional thumping from the bedroom followed by the giggle of girls who were not sleeping.

"It's like a slumber party here every night," said his mom.

"They happy here?"

"Seem to be. They ask about their mother and what's going to happen."

Kee knew that the foster girls' mother had been arrested on drug charges and not for the first time. This time it was more serious because she had been caught with quantities that meant she was either dealing or transporting illegal substances. She likely would do federal time.

"They miss their big sister, Kacey. She practically raised them, with her mother gone and now we know where. Delivering drugs." His mother made a tsking sound. "The youngest, Shirley, still steals food."

"Steals?" he asked.

"She's still not quite sure there will be a next meal."

Kee's heart broke at the news. "So what do you do?"

"Let her steal it, if it makes her feel better. She'll get over it in time. Being hungry is hard and it isn't something you can just get past because someone says so."

Kee had never been that hungry. Even when their father had been in jail or off for weeks at a time, his mother always had a meal on the table. He wondered now how she had managed.

"Abbie and Shirley are becoming best friends, though Winnie is closer to her age."

"I'm glad they have you, Mom."

She flushed and smiled, waving away the compliment as if keeping three more girls fed and safe and loved was no big deal.

"How's your leg?" he asked. His mom had diabetes and was recovering from an open wound on her ankle where she'd nicked the coffee table.

"All healed. They got me wearing special stockings now. But don't change the subject. You said two reasons for not having her arrested and you gave me one. What's the other?"

Now Kee flushed.

"Oh, I see. You like her, despite the fact that she was playing you."

"That's about it."

"You got anything to be ashamed of, son?"

He looked startled and felt about fifteen again. He met her gaze.

"Kee?"

"No, ma'am."

"Well, then she'll figure that out eventually. And you can't blame her for protecting her own. Think what you'd be prepared to do if Abbie went missing."

That thought made his stomach frost and caused a pain in his heart. What had Ava been going through?

"You're right," he answered. "But I think her interest in me centers on her investigation."

"Maybe it did. But now that she's met you, her interests might change."

She rose heavily from her seat, using her arms

and the armrests to help hoist her upright. Then she shuffled over to him, stooped to kiss his forehead. "Good night, son. Thank you for giving up your bedroom for the girls."

Kee followed her as far as the living room and watched her slow progress down the hall. His mother had raised all her children, except his little sister, who was still under her roof. Now she also had three foster girls and he wondered if it might be too much.

He settled on the couch, slipping between the folded blanket and sheet on the sagging cushions that had barely survived the raising of four hopping, bouncing boys. He closed his eyes, certain that he would not sleep. He thought of Ava and all she had told him. His mother was right. She had a duty to look for her niece and if that meant lying to him, he could at least understand the whys of it. Even if he didn't like it.

The following morning he was up, washed and dressed as the girls poured into the kitchen for breakfast. He knew that he did not want to be stuck in line for the bathroom behind four girls.

His mother kissed him goodbye and whispered that he should be careful. Because of his early departure, he had time to walk down by the river before the clinic opened and speak to Jake, who was on traffic duty there again.

Most of the residents of Piñon Flats were returning today and some were making several trips with pickups hastily packed. Traffic was heavy. Kee pulled his pickup to the shoulder and stood in the road with Jake, who was acting as a human stop signal in a place that never needed one until today.

"Hey, big brother," said Jake. "How are things?"

He was tempted to tell him exactly how things were but instead he stuck to the purpose of his visit. He wasn't all right. And things had never been worse.

"Do you know Ava Hood?" he asked.

Jake kept his attention on his work but he nodded. "She's our new hire."

A truck rolled past and Jake stopped the next one, motioning for the perpendicular lane of traffic to proceed.

"Have you seen her?"

Jake shook his head. "Never met."

"Did you know she's up here investigating my clinic?"

"Where'd you hear that?"

"From her." Kee quickly told him what Ava had shared.

"I can't really talk about this, Kee. You understand?" Another line of vehicles rolled past, some with their windows down and the driver's elbows resting on the open window frames. Most waved or called a greeting. He stopped the line for the arrival of a huge dump truck and their conversation resumed.

"I gave her access to the records of each girl's visit. The visits all have my name on them."

Jake's arms dropped. "They do?"

"But I didn't see them. I don't understand. He said he wants me to follow his footsteps and take over our clinic one day. Then he implicates me."

"Maybe he was hoping to include you in his illegal activities, too."

"I would never…"

"So when things started to get hot and he had to choose him or you, well…"

Kee grimaced.

"He couldn't use Day's name. He wasn't here long enough to be involved."

Jake's rational made him feel simultaneously better and worse.

"According to Ava, Lori figured out the connection when you were investigating the missing girls. Why did they give you that assignment? You're first year. A rookie."

"I can't talk about cases with you. But I can say that I took on extra responsibilities when Jack Bear Den was handling the eco-extremists attack on the dam case and the evacuation. So I was asked to interview a few families and responded to a few calls that normally would have been his. I'd been out to see most of the families before the girls went missing, on escort with protective services or for disturbance calls. Big families, single-parent families."

Jake began waving traffic forward again, his arms sweeping in graceful circles.

"Did your daughter arrive in your care before or after this?"

"Kee, you need to be careful. If you think something is happening at your clinic, you should go to Tinnin or Bear Den."

"Is Ty in trouble?"

"Yes."

"What kind?"

"I can't say."

"Damn it, Jake."

The dump truck made it off the road and into the construction site. Jake waved on the waiting traffic.

He cast Kee a pained look as his hand continued a rhythmic sweep. "He took Kacey…" He shook his head. "She wanted to be taken and they sent Ty."

"Who?"

Jake gave him an exasperated look and his hand waved faster. Kee wasn't sure if he was impatient for the traffic to move or with his big brother.

"The gang?"

"I'm not sure if wanted is the right way of saying it. Ty told Kacey that Colt sent him and Colt *was* there when she arrived."

"But…?"

"Kacey went to our clinic to be captured. You understand? She showed up and was picked up again right on our rez. Evidence leads us to believe Ty was the pickup man and Kacey's statement corroborates.

Only reason he's not in jail is that in Colt's statement—" Jake stopped. "I can't talk about this. Point is, we couldn't find the others and Kacey hoped to lead the FBI to the new location where her friends had been taken because they moved them after she escaped."

"So was Ty helping her or helping the gang?"

"That's the question. Maybe both." Jake pushed his cowboy hat back on his head, making him look younger and less intimidating.

"And Ty was the pickup man?" asked Kee.

"Kacey knew him. Colt's big brother. He'd be the logical one for the Wolf Posse to send because she'd trust him. Get in the car with him."

"But she wanted to be captured?" Kee said, echoing Jake's words.

"The Wolf Posse couldn't have known that," said Jake as traffic continued to roll past, referring to the tribe's gang.

"True," Kee said.

More vehicles rolled by. Several called a greeting in Tonto.

"Listen, I'll tell you something else about Ty. The only reason I'm not dead is because he knew that the gang sent two kidnappers after us. To get Fortune, you understand? He was there. He and Hemi… you know Hemi?"

"Hemi also found Richard's body."

"I heard that."

"I didn't know any of this. I'm sorry, Jake, that I wasn't there for you."

Jake looked at Kee. "Are you mixed up in this, Kee?"

"No. I swear."

"I'll help you all I can. Be careful at work. I'm sure that someone killed your coworker."

Jake hugged him and then Kee headed back to his truck more troubled than he had been since his father's sentencing.

Kee had played by every rule and guarded his reputation fiercely, and yet he still found himself implicated. How could something like this happen?

Chapter Twelve

Despite Kee's detour, he made it to the clinic nearly forty-five minutes early. He pulled his truck behind the building, parking in his usual place before tribal headquarters. He liked this spot because it had shade all day from the large pines planted long ago. It did require him to walk across the road that divided the two buildings, behind the women's health wing windows and around the side of the building where he usually entered through the women's clinic entrance, or, if he arrived before the clinic opened, through the break-room-side entrance beyond. As he rounded the corner to the break room, he spotted an unfamiliar black dually pickup with Arizona plates pull up on the sidewalk.

Hector emerged from the clinic's break room door followed by Betty, who carried something in her hands. Kee paused as he wondered what was going on.

Hector and Betty stood not ten feet away from Kee as a white man exited the truck. The man was thin and muscular and wore motorcycle boots, jeans and a green T-shirt. His short brown hair seemed vaguely military in style. His arms were covered from his sleeve to his wrist with blue-black tattoos including circular bands on each bicep depicting a linked chain punctuated by a skull design. A tattooed dagger dripping blood appeared to pass from one side of his clavicle, through his neck, and emerge out the other. He also had a long series of gouges on his right arm that dripped pus.

Hauser was speaking to the man and handed over what Kee recognized as a Z-pak. Zithromax was an antibiotic used to treat bacterial infections like the ones on the man's arms. But this clinic only treated tribe members. There was something off about this and all Ava's suppositions about his clinic rose up in his mind.

The man glanced up, spotted Kee and reached behind him. Kee had the distinct feeling he was going for a gun. Kee called out to Hector. "Need any help?"

Betty spun about and Hauser glanced over his shoulder at Kee and then pressed a hand to the man's forearm, speaking in a tone too low for Kee to hear. Then he smiled at Kee.

"Kee, my boy." Then he turned to Betty. "See to him, will you?"

Betty dropped the gauze roll into Hector's hand before hurrying across the sidewalk to intercept Kee.

"What's going on?" asked Kee.

"The guy was sent over by FEMA. One of the construction workers."

"Why isn't he inside?"

"Because he refused to come in. Claustrophobic or afraid of hospitals. Who knows?" She tossed up her hands and retrieved the key she had on a pink plastic spiral bracelet. She unlocked the women's clinic doors and shooed him inside. "Glad to get away from him. He gives me the creeps."

She followed him inside and breathed a sigh of relief, then locked the door. Then she peered out. "You think Hector will be all right?"

Kee stood beside Betty but he could no longer see the patient. "You want me to go out?"

A moment later the truck roared past. The man turned to fix Kee with a hard look through the clinic windows.

"See, he's loco," said Betty and then turned to him. "You're here awful early."

"Trying to beat the Doka girls to the bathroom."

Betty laughed. "That's right. You've moved back home again. Want me to make some calls? See if I can get you something temporary?"

"That would be great."

She patted his arm, making her gold bracelets chime, and then headed toward her office at the main reception area in the urgent care wing of their clinic.

It wasn't until he was halfway back to the break room that he recalled what Ava had said the evening they found Day's body. That his death was no accident and there was blood and skin under Day's nails.

Hauser said that all the injuries were consistent with a fall. But if Ava was right, then this man, the one with the tattoos, could be the one who pushed Richard off that cliff.

He pondered the wounds he had seen on the stranger's arms. Long gouges. Kee curled his fingers into a claw and imagined raking it down a man's arm. Yes, that was what they'd look like.

Kee stood frozen in the hallway. Should he tell Ava or call his brother Jake?

He lifted his phone and dialed Ava.

"What did he look like?" she asked.

He described the man in as much detail as he could.

"Describe the tattoos again."

He did.

"We have a database for tattoos. Let me make a call and see what I can come up with."

"Ava, if it is Hector and he has your name, that guy might come after you next."

There was silence on the line. Was that her plan all along, to use herself as bait?

"What can I do to help?"

"Treat your patients, Kee, and don't do anything that would alert Hauser that you are suspicious."

That was certainly easier said than done.

"And text me when you are done. I want to meet you somewhere private."

"We have a tribal compound. It's private."

"Okay. Just tell me how to get there."

BETTY SPOKE TO Hector from her seat at the receptionist desk between patients who were waiting beyond the glass partition or scribbling in the boxes on their forms.

"You remember I set a trigger after Kacey Doka showed up, to see if anyone accessed her file or any of the packages we sent over?" she asked.

"Yes." He wasn't as good as Betty at keeping the worry from showing. Since Kacey Doka had escaped they'd been in defense mode. They had two more "packages" ready, but knew they'd both be missed now that tribal police suspected that the runaways were actually abducted. What would happen when they figured out they were pregnant?

"Well, it went off."

Turning her attention back to her receptionist duties, Betty smiled at Mr. Imperius, who slid the clipboard through the slot. "Thank you, Andy. It will be just a few more minutes." She held that smile until Andy turned his back and lumbered back to his chair. She followed him with her eyes. "His color isn't good."

"What about the trigger? Who was it?" asked Hector.

Betty spun to face him and gave him the name.

"Kee Redhorse."

Hector's jaw dropped. "No."

"I've already made the call."

"No. Let's wait a minute. It could be…"

She rested a hand on his and gave a squeeze, bringing his attention back to her. Her dark eyes met his.

"There's no mistake. Avangeline Yokota is a detective, she found Richard's body and now she's gotten Kee to log in to our system."

"But you can't see anything there. It's just appointments."

"It's enough. Kee knows he didn't treat those girls. I'll call Yury. He'll take care of it."

Hector rocked forward and only just caught himself on his knuckles, cracking the clipboard beneath his fist.

"Like he took care of Day?" whispered Hauser. "They took tissue samples from Day. I couldn't stop them. They have Yury's physical evidence."

"So they'll have a suspect."

"A Russian mobster. He's been in prison. Why would he push Day?"

"It doesn't matter as long as it doesn't come back to us. He's an outsider. Plus he'll never betray his bosses. That would be suicide."

"Kee." Hauser shook his head.

"Who knows what he's been doing?" said Betty. "I know for a fact that he saw me with at least one pregnancy test," said Betty. "Back in February with Marta Garcia, and I am not sure that he bought my story that it was standard for us to take this precaution in young women with certain markers in their medical history. He'll think back on that. If he knows we are involved with the missing girls, he might figure it out. Plus he saw Yury outside this morning."

He laid a hand on her shoulder. "Yury pushing Day. It's made it worse. Now we have a detective sniffing around. Kee saw him, and Louisa is the detective's niece. He might do something to point to us."

"The only one who has seen him with us is Kee."

"This is bad." He started to pace.

"Hector," she hissed. "You have patients. I called Yury again. Don't worry."

"But Kee. He's not involved."

"He is now. She's using him to get to us. You know that."

"But Kee. I've been grooming him."

"Hector, it's your life's work. Your legacy. Remember that."

"Excuse me?" said a female voice at the window counter.

Betty turned to face Lucinda Olive, a warm smile fixed on her face. Lucinda was full-blood Apache, spoke the language perfectly and held her young feverish son in her arms.

"Uriah is feeling like he might be sick."

Betty rose. "Well, that makes two of you."

"What?" said Lucinda.

"Bring him in, dear. Dr. Hauser will see him right away."

AVA CALLED KEE from the parking lot of tribal headquarters, right next to the clinic.

"I've got information on the tattoos you saw and

some images. They photograph prisoners and their tattoos. Have you got a minute to come out and see me?"

Kee had patients waiting but he headed for the break room and then stepped out the back to meet Ava, who sat in her Chevy with the laptop booted up. He slipped into the passenger seat.

"I don't want them to know I'm gone."

"I'll be quick. I have them narrowed down."

She placed the laptop between them and began flicking through photos of neck tattoos.

"No," he said to the first and the next three she showed him. On the fourth he pointed. "That's it. It looked like this."

"Exactly like it or similar?"

"Seems the same."

She regained possession of the laptop and clicked away.

"That particular tattoo is favored by Russian mobsters. It means he is a hired killer. It's like a billboard advertising his specialty."

"Doesn't that make him easier to catch?" asked Kee.

"Unfortunately tattoos like this are just indicators, not evidence."

She placed the laptop between them again, showing him several other tattoos.

"I didn't see his hands or…what is that, his back?"

She clicked to the next photo. There, looking out at him with a face filled with sullen rage was a white man with his head shaved, square jaw lifted and neck tattoo clearly visible.

"That's him."

"You sure?"

"A hundred percent."

She glanced at the screen, scanning. "His name is Yury Churkin. He works for Leonard Usov, who is his Avtoritet, or authority, like a captain. They both belong to the Kuznetsov crime family out of Atlanta. Narcotics, money laundering and human trafficking. They run strip clubs and various businesses catering to the hospitality business."

"Hospitality?" asked Kee.

"Prostitution."

"Usov likely runs all the kidnapping rings in this region. Churkin is just muscle. A killer. He was here for Day. I still don't know why. But I need you to get Betty away from her office for a few minutes so I can get my camera and take a look at the footage."

"What footage?"

"I placed a camera above her computer so I can grab her passwords. It's been running all day."

Kee gaped. "You broke in?"

"Actually one of the nurses let me in. It was easy to tape the door so I could get back in after she went back to the nursery."

"That's breaking and entering."

"It sure is. So, can you get me into the clinic later so I can access her computer?"

Kee's jaw hardened. "I'm not sure how to do that.

Betty stays pretty close to her desk. Even eats lunch there."

"Do you have any patients in the women's health clinic?"

"Not today. The one newborn has gone home with her family."

"So all patients are in the reception area or exam rooms?"

He nodded.

"What about a fire alarm?"

Kee went pale. "You want me to pull a false alarm?"

"Yes. Or get me inside and I'll pull it."

He blinked at her and then scrubbed his hand over his mouth. He spoke more to himself than to her. "It's against the law."

"So is kidnapping young women."

"You're going with the ends justifying the means. Is that it?" he challenged.

"Whatever gets that alarm pulled," she countered.

He met her gaze and she waited as the seconds ticked and he battled with his conscience. "You saw Churkin. You saw the scratches. You saw Day's body. Kee, this is happening right here at your clinic."

"I could call Jake or the chief."

"It could take them weeks to get what I can in a few minutes."

"Because they'll do it legally."

Her searing gaze never wavered. "They have my niece."

He sighed, knowing he was going to help her even as his inner rule-follower screamed *don't!* "I'll get you in the break room. Then I'll pull the alarm. But only after I am sure there are no patients in the exam rooms and no one will get hurt."

She looked impressed. "Sounds good."

"When?"

"Now."

Chapter Thirteen

Ava slipped into the break room and waited as Kee continued on out into the corridor. Had she convinced him? Did he now see what she saw? It hurt her to know that she had caused him to see just what was happening here, but she was relieved to know that Kee was not involved.

Unless he was playing her and now she was here in the break room with no backup and just her personal service weapon. She thought of the Russian, Yury Churkin. The man was a cold-blooded killer and even with all her training, she would not want to face him. Ava glanced toward the door, considering escape. Why had she trusted Kee? She knew better than to rely on anyone.

She shouldn't let her physical reaction to Kee sway her. Shouldn't let her breath catch or her heart ache. Shouldn't have to battle the urge to stroke his broad chest or notice the way the concern caused a deep line to form between his brows.

Every time she was near him, Ava took the opportunity to breathe in his rich, enticing scent. Kee smelled of mint and some exotic earthy fragrance like teak. There were traces of him here still in the air all about her. She was losing her battle not to touch him every time she got near him.

She hovered by the window, considering escape as the minutes dragged by endlessly.

When the siren sounded she exhaled a long breath and stared at the ceiling. It was so hard not knowing whom to trust.

He'd done it. The doctor who played all things by the rules had just pulled a false alarm in his clinic. Kee ducked his head into the room and nodded.

"All clear."

She walked quickly down the hall, passing Radiology, and then turned left to the lobby and the reception area. Betty Mills's office. It was locked. The woman had locked the door behind her upon leaving. Smart. That move only made Ava more certain about Mills. Ava stared up at the one smoke detector beyond the glass partition that was not sounding because it was not a detector, but did hold a tiny camera pointing straight down at Betty's keyboard. She had activated it remotely this morning as Betty arrived.

Ava used her locksmith kit to work on the door. It was a simple latch with no deadbolt. Relatively easy to pick, except her heart was hammering and her hand shook. The volunteer fire department was right next to tribal police and would be here any second. She heard the tumblers click at the same time she heard the front door open.

She ducked inside and closed the door, using the wall between the lobby and this office as cover as the fire department crew entered. She heard them moving down the hall and away from her position. She calculated it would take them only a few minutes to check each room for smoke.

Ava was quick as a cat as she leaped up onto Betty's desk. She yanked the detector down and tossed it in her bag. Then she headed out of the office, pressing the lock button before drawing the door softly closed. She followed the route the men would have taken, planning to stay behind them. Down the hall past Hauser's office she went, turning at exam room number one and the supply closet, where she turned right. She made it to the end of the next short hall and faced the procedure room. The men had already passed Radiology and were heading to the women's health clinic when Ava ducked out the door that led to a courtyard and tribal headquarters and right into Chief Wallace Tinnin.

"Just the person I was looking for," said the chief.

Tinnin stood with hands on his crutch grips, his chin dipped and his brows lifted, giving her a look from under the brim of his cowboy hat that one might cast an unmanageable child. She could almost see the storm clouds forming over his head.

"I'm going to need you to come with me."

She followed him across the courtyard and into the side entrance of tribal headquarters. She trailed behind him down the corridor, the extra weight of the smoke detector heavy in her bag. He clicked slowly along on the crutches. So she took the opportunity to open the detector and remove the camera and SIM card. These she slipped into her bra. If he was arresting her, then it wouldn't make any difference. She knew that Chief Tinnin would not use the information on the recorder to break into Betty Mills's computer because he followed the letter of the law and she had not completely ruled out the possibly that he was working with the clinic. But she was leaning toward taking him at face value. Tinnin appeared to be a good man and good cop who was overworked and understaffed.

He opened the door to the squad room and she marched past Carol Dorset, the dispatcher. The woman lifted her penciled eyebrows at Ava and returned to her call, taking down an address in a log.

She walked before the chief past the four desks, only one of which was occupied by Detective Jack Bear Den, who rose as she passed. He spoke to the chief.

"You found her."

"Wasn't hard. Just followed the sounds of sirens."

The two men waited for her to enter the chief's office. Tinnin rounded his ancient desk and motioned to the wooden chair. Bear Den closed the door with a snap and stood behind her.

At least she wasn't in the single interrogation room…yet.

Behind Tinnin on the full bookshelf were rows of empty moving boxes. His desk was clear except for the phone, computer and a rusty spur atop a stack of files. She narrowed her eyes on the object that seemed to belong in a scrap heap.

"You pull that alarm?" asked Tinnin.

"No, sir."

"You know who did?"

She said nothing. Tinnin's mouth tipped down at both corners.

He took off his hat, threw it to the coatrack and missed. He swore and lifted the hat from the floor with his crutch and lowered it to the hook. Then he took a seat.

"We have the autopsy reports."

"Reports? Plural?"

"Yes, ma'am. First is from Hauser." He retrieved a page from a file and set the report before her, turning it to face her. "Says accidental death as a result of a fall."

She lifted her brows. "But what caused the fall?"

"Hauser doesn't speculate. But he also did not note the blood and skin cells under the deceased person's nails. You noted them in the dark, I recall."

"You have samples?" she asked.

"The ME took them before Hauser arrived." Tinnin nodded. "Do you have any?"

"No, sir."

"The FBI is expediting the test results. Nothing yet. I'm listing the death as a homicide, but not making that public knowledge."

It was not the sort of thing a police chief would

tell someone if he was involved in a cover-up. Was he collaborating with her?

"I see."

"You wondering why I'm letting you run around loose on my rez?"

"It occurred to me."

"Because you're doing what I can't. I'm sure you'll lose your badge. That's the best outcome. But in the meantime, if you don't get killed, you might just find me something I can use."

She already had. The tissue sample the ME collected was hard evidence that Day had not fallen.

Her phone chimed. She glanced at the screen to the text from Kee.

Where are u?

Did u get it?

She texted back.

Got it and am out. Call u later.

TINNIN WATCHED HER with a level gaze, his face revealing nothing. The fact that he did not stop her from reading or sending text messages was another point in his favor.

"Why isn't Ty Redhorse in jail?" she asked.

"On what charge?"

"He drove Kacey Doka to an isolated spot and

turned her over to two men, one of whom is still in the hospital paralyzed."

"All true."

"So why isn't he in jail?"

"Because it's unclear if Ty was protecting her or kidnapping her."

"He brought her to her captors."

"Which was her intention when she left protective custody, to lead the FBI to her captors and her friends. Ty alerted his brother Colt, who called us. He and Colt took proactive action to ensure Kacey's escape."

"But then, is Ty working with the gang or with you?"

Tinnin waved away her question. "Ongoing investigation."

That was bullshit. She knew it and so did he. Whatever the reason, he wasn't telling her. And he didn't have to. She was no longer a detective working a case. She'd gone rogue and he owed her nothing. With the situation reversed, she'd have said the exact same thing.

Ava suggested, deciding to trust the chief with what she knew, "Check the tissue samples against Yury Churkin, if you can."

Tinnin opened his desk drawer and Ava braced for what he might draw from within. He hadn't taken her weapon and she planned to use it if she needed to. Detective Bear Den looked ready to do the same.

The drawer was empty. Tinnin swore and looked at the boxes on the floor. "Don't even have a damn pencil."

"Use your cell phone," said Bear Den. "Take a note there."

Tinnin drew out his phone and punched at an app, typing in the name she had offered.

"How did you get that name?" he asked.

She told them about the man that Kee had seen this morning before the clinic opened and watched Tinnin's reaction. Her best guess was that he had not known. If he was in on this, he should have.

"We don't treat outsiders," said Bear Den.

"Well, Hauser just did."

"We need to get Kee in here," said Tinnin to Bear Den.

Ava lifted a hand. "You might not want to march him into police headquarters. Maybe send his brother to talk to him. It would seem less suspicious."

Tinnin and Bear Den had a silent exchange and Bear Den nodded and left.

"Was that a yes?" she asked.

"We'll be discreet. And you be careful. Keep that pistol handy, wear your vest and call me if you see Churkin again."

"Yes, sir."

She rose and the chief gave her a long steady look.

"It's a shame because I really would have enjoyed working with you, Detective."

AFTER COMFORTING SARA, Ava had called Sara's mother-in-law and explained the situation. Sylavania Tah was a widow in her midsixties. She was extremely overweight, and suffered from numerous health issues including high blood pressure, gout and diabetes. But she did love her grandbabies, and Ava knew they would be safe with her.

Ava no longer trusted Sara alone with her kids, but she did want to help her. So on Thursday morning, after Sara had sobered up, Ava had given her sister an ultimatum. She got help or Ava would petition the tribe for custody of her girls. Ava had reminded Sara about their mother's closet drinking and the auto accident when Ava was eleven and Sara fourteen. It had caused their mom to take oxycodone for the pain and the next thing they knew, Mom was using heroin and they were in foster care.

Sara had, at least, been willing to admit she had a problem. Their mom had been in denial until she contracted Hepatitis C.

In the afternoon, Ava took Sara to her first AA meeting. Ava was not optimistic by nature but she hoped Sara could turn it around. When they got back to the trailer, they started packing, tossed all the stashed liquor in the trash and switched Sara to iced coffee. It was going to be a rough couple of days at the Tah household.

She texted Kee and asked him to call her but he sent a text back with a two-word reply.

With Patients

She helped her sister move back into her home. It took three trips from Turquoise Ridge to Piñon Flats, in two cars. Afterward, Ava helped Sara clean up until Sara went to pick up the girls at school.

The following day, Sara went food shopping in the afternoon and Ava picked up her nieces from their former school building, which had reopened today. She started dinner when she began to worry. Sara's usual schedule was to stay sober until the girls were home and then start drinking until she passed out on the sofa. But Sara wasn't home yet.

She dialed Sara's phone and got voice mail. Just before 6:30 p.m. there was a knock at the door. She thought it would be Kee, but instead found Officer Wetselline standing on the step, his face grim.

"What happened?" Ava asked.

"There's been an accident."

Chapter Fourteen

Ava waited until the girls' paternal grandmother arrived at a little past eight. Sara's mother-in-law had packed an overnight bag and was prepared to stay for a day or two but Ava assured her that she'd be back tonight.

"Just preparing. Last time I had them for nearly two weeks."

Ava's mouth gaped. "I had no idea."

Her frightened nieces wanted to know why their mother was not home.

"She's been in an accident," said Ava. "But she's all right."

"Was she sober again?" asked Alexandra, getting the words mixed up. Ava did not think a five-year-old should even have to know the difference between the words *drunk* and *sober*.

"She drove her car into a ditch. I'm going to see her now."

Margarita began to cry and her twin followed suit. Olivia gripped Ava's leg.

"You come back?" asked the three-year-old.

Ava dropped to a knee to hug her. "I will come back."

The grandmother got the girls all back to the table and Ava set out to tribal police headquarters.

When she'd come here she had thought that she

was unencumbered. That she was risking her job and possibly making some moves that could land her in jail or worse. She'd accepted all those risks, even given her name to Hauser, hoping to draw him out. But now she saw her mistake.

She wasn't free and what happened to her *did* matter, because of Sara's children. She had come here to rescue Louisa, only to discover that all of Sara's children needed a rescue. And if Ava was being targeted by Hauser, if he called in his Russian killers or the tribe's gang and something happened to Ava…what then? She would be leaving her nieces with an alcoholic mother and a grandmother who was in very poor health. Worse still, those girls gave her exactly the kind of vulnerability that could be used against her. Worse still, her enemies might attack Sara and her girls directly or try to use them against her.

What had she done?

If she could go back, she would have brought what she learned to Chief Tinnin. But now it was too late for that. The only way out was through and she prayed this did not touch Olivia, Margarita and Alexandra.

Ava called Jack Bear Den from the driveway of her sister's home. He did not diminish her worry but took what she said so seriously that it gave her chills. He agreed to stake out her sister's house until she got back. She waited thirty minutes for him to arrive before departing. She didn't like trusting the safety of her sister's family to anyone else, but the alternative of leaving them unprotected was not an option.

She reached the police station a few minutes before nine and was met by Jake Redhorse. He'd been the first on scene. He brought her to the jail cell, where Ava found Sara sound asleep on a cot, with a bandaged nose and two black eyes.

"I took her to her first AA meeting yesterday."

"Blood alcohol was 0.15. She'll be arraigned in tribal court on Monday morning. No bail until then. Ava, who's got her kids?"

"Grandmother." *And Jack Bear Den*, she thought.

Redhorse nodded. "I've called protective services. They'll be around sometime tomorrow. I don't think Sara can take care of them for a while."

"Their grandmother…"

Redhorse looked away. "How's she doing?"

"She's…ill."

"Not going to be able to handle three kids all under six. Right?"

Ava changed the subject. "What do you think Sara will get? Bail? Release on recognizance?"

Redhorse made a face. "It's not her first offense. And she's driving on a suspended license."

"What?" Ava had no idea.

"She's going to do some time. I'm guessing three months."

Now Ava looked away. "I'll take them."

But first she was going to find their older sister, Louisa.

"Tell Sara I was here. Will you?"

Redhorse nodded and showed her out.

Ava left the jail and headed out. She now had Betty's passwords and she was anxious to try them. She sent Kee a text and he called back.

"Where are you?" he asked.

The concern in his voice was the tipping point. Her throat constricted and the tears came, wetting her cheeks. She wanted to tell him about Sara and how worried she was about the safety of her nieces. She wanted to tell him that she was afraid her investigation would backfire on them and that might just kill her. Instead she told him where she was and asked him for another favor that could cost him his job.

"The break room window?" he asked.

"Yes. Just leave it cracked before you go."

"Now?"

"Yes." She held her breath, waiting for him to decide. He'd already shared medical records with her and pulled a fire alarm to give her access to Betty's office. The fact that he would do things so contrary to his nature showed either how disturbed he was by what was happening at his workplace or how much he trusted her. Maybe both.

She couldn't get caught. If she was discovered in the building, Hauser's first suspect would be Kee.

"I'll leave it open."

"Thank you. I couldn't do this without you."

"Will I see you later?" he asked.

"Yes."

And he was gone. Ava made mental preparations. Breaking in was impossibly simple thanks to Kee leaving the break room window unlocked and cracked enough for her to get her fingers underneath. Once inside she retraced her footsteps of earlier in the day and again picked the lock to Mills's door. Without the pressure of time, she managed the lock on the first try. She logged in to Betty's terminal a little after 10 p.m., had Betty's hard drive copied and was out the door before eleven with the flash drive in hand. With luck she'd have the files duplicated and a copy into Tinnin's hands this evening.

She made it to her car and was heading toward her sister's home when her phone chimed with an incoming call from Kee. She pulled over and picked up.

"I just heard about Sara."

"How?"

"Jake phoned me. You all right?"

"Not really. Sara is in jail."

"Where are the girls?"

"With their grandmother."

"Alone?"

"Tribal is keeping watch."

She heard Kee exhale into the speaker in a sound that seemed like relief.

"Where are you?"

"En route to Sara's place."

"I'm coming over."

Her first response was no. It was how she answered most invitations. But she discovered that she wanted Kee there with her tonight so much she ached with need.

Still, she said, "No. It's dangerous. Hauser has my name. He should have figured out who I am by now."

"If you think you are in danger, you shouldn't be there with the girls or alone."

"Tribal police is there."

"And in a few minutes, I will be, as well."

It broke her heart to say the next part. "protective services is coming tomorrow. I'd turn them over for their own safety, but I don't think they can protect them from this. I don't know where else to take them. I've made a terrible mistake."

"Call Chief Tinnin."

"Detective Bear Den is there. But they can't watch over us forever."

"His fiancée is still up here. She's FBI."

"That might work. Temporarily."

"I'm on my way to you."

Her heart gave a lurch of anticipation and squeezed as worry mingled with relief. She could count on Kee. She knew it.

"Don't. It's not safe."

Kee hung up on her. She reeled in the hurt she had no right to feel at this rejection.

AVA CONTINUED TOWARD her sister's place in Piñon Flats. She slowed as she neared the house, and pulled up beside Bear Den's unit and explained that she was ready to call the FBI for help. He called his fiancée and FBI Field Agent Sophia Rivas called her boss, an agent named Luke Forrest.

Bear Den waited out front while Ava met Sylavania at the door and explained what she knew about Sara's situation. Sara's mother-in-law had known that Sara had one DUI within the year. Everyone knew, apparently, because her mug shot had been in the tribal newspaper and, worse still, Sara had been arrested off the rez so she'd faced the Arizona county court system.

"You know I'd be pleased to take them," said Sylavania.

History repeating itself, thought Ava. Their mom had had Sara at fifteen and Ava at eighteen and then left them with their grandmother to run off to Oklahoma with some tour guy. Her mom hadn't returned until Ava was seven. Then she'd come home to stay with them, hiding her drinking for a while. But after Ava's grandmother died, her mom's drinking had gotten much worse.

This was exactly what Ava had been trying to prevent and here it was happening anyway.

"Wouldn't it be difficult because of your health issues?" Ava asked.

Sylavania drew her mouth into a tight line and looked away. "I'd manage."

Ava admired her spirit. "We'll talk about it to-morrow."

And tomorrow she'd tell Sylavania that the girls were in FBI protective custody. She doubted their grandmother would forgive her.

"Are you sure you don't want me to stay?"

So sure, she thought. The sooner Sylavania got home the sooner she'd be out of the crosshairs.

"I'll call if I need a break. How will that be?"

"Yes, that will work." Sylavania gathered her bag and her keys. "Speak to you tomorrow, sometime."

Sylavania took Ava's hand. "Sara and the girls are so lucky to have you."

Ava felt the stab of guilt. She'd put them in danger in her bid to find Louisa. Now she had to get help to keep them safe.

Ava saw her out and watched the woman struggle to her car and drop into her seat. The car's springs sagged. That woman had a full heart, but Ava could see the future. She didn't want her nieces in the custody of a grandmother who would not live to see them grown. What she wanted was for her sister to get sober and take responsibility for her children. But that would be up to protective services. In the short-term, Ava meant to see that her search for Louisa did not endanger her other nieces. That meant getting Margarita, Alexandra and Olivia to safety.

Sylavania passed Bear Den as she pulled out,

though she doubted the woman noticed his cruiser parked just off the road in a neighbor's drive.

Ava wanted to get to the computer records, but first she'd see her nieces safe. She did not have long to wait. Bear Den was at her door with a woman who identified herself as FBI field agent Sophia Rivas. She was a beautiful woman with an athletic build and a serious no-nonsense expression. Her clothing was practical and Ava saw she preferred a shoulder holster, as well.

They agreed to take the girls to a safe house for the night in exchange for Ava's full cooperation in the morning.

"You should come with us," said Rivas.

"I have some work."

Rivas gave her a hard look. "We could be working together, you know."

She shook her head. She knew the FBI was investigating the connection between the tribe's missing women and the Russian crime family operating out of Atlanta. They'd likely make a case, but it would take months. Months that Louisa did not have.

"You are not the only one working here. Not the only one who cares and certainly not the only one hurt by these disappearances. It's not an excuse to go vigilante."

"Just take care of the girls."

"That I will do. And you take care of yourself, because you seem incapable of letting anyone else near you. Must be very lonely in that tower where you live."

Ava set her jaw and glared. What right did this woman have to come in here and judge her?

She showed them both back to the girls' room. Olivia did not even wake when Ava took her from her bed and set her in the car seat now in the back of Bear Den's cruiser, but Margarita and Alexandra were both scared and crying when the three girls were driven away in Bear Den's police unit. Ava could see them in the rear car seats and in her mind's eye she could see Sara and herself being driven away that first time when Mom was assigned mandatory drug rehab for the oxycodone. How had she let this happen?

She was still staring after them even though they were out of sight when a dark truck appeared on the road.

Ava switched off the light behind her and ducked down. Was it Churkin?

The truck slowed and Ava drew her weapon. With a flick of one finger she had the safety off.

The truck pulled into Sara's drive. It was not the sort of move a killer would make. Ava hazarded a quick look at the vehicle. It was an older model dark blue RAM pickup.

Kee.

Ava stood on the step as Kee stepped out of the truck. He spotted her just after rounding the hood and smiled.

"I told you not to come over," she said.

He ignored her as he closed the door with a thud.

"And I'm no better at following orders than my patients."

She hesitated, wanting so badly to run to him and throw herself into his arms.

"You're not the only one who can break the rules. And I can make up my own mind about what I choose to do. And I wanted to see you."

Up until pulling that fire alarm, Kee had not been the sort of man to color outside the lines. She liked it but she didn't want him hurt because of her.

He opened his arms to her and she threw herself against him. His arms enfolded her as she squeezed her eyes shut tight, overwhelmed at the joy that came from his strong arms around her.

"It's dangerous," she whispered. "Your being here."

"You don't want to put me in danger?"

"Of course not."

"But you're in danger."

She nodded.

"Then more reason that I'm staying."

He dropped a kiss on her forehead and then her cheek. She lifted her chin, offering her lips. The quicksilver reaction of his mouth brushing hers took her breath away. In a moment she was deepening the kiss as her heart jackhammered in her chest. He placed his hands on her shoulders and then swept them down to her lower back, bringing them together at the hip. Nothing ever felt so right. But there were too many layers of clothing between her and him. She wanted—no, needed—to feel his skin gliding over hers.

She drew back to reach for the buttons on his shirt and stopped herself. They were still standing on the stoop before her sister's house. Ava dropped her hands to her sides.

"You should go."

He never took his hungry eyes off her as he spoke. "I won't, though. So let me in or I'll camp on your front step."

Ava glanced at the street and saw nothing and no one.

She stepped aside and Kee swept past her. She followed him, locking the door behind them.

Chapter Fifteen

The familiar musical melody of his cell phone woke Hector before it could repeat. He was as used to being awakened from a sound sleep to handle medical emergencies as his wife was to sleeping through such calls. She rolled to her side and made a gurgling sound as he answered.

"This is Dr. Hauser," he said, his voice gravelly. He'd been asleep just long enough to feel dim-witted.

"Someone logged on to my terminal," said a familiar female voice.

He knew the voice immediately. It was Betty Mills calling him at home. She never called him at home. Not ever. At this time of night, all emergency calls came from the volunteer fire department. His heart was hammering as he spun to an upright position.

"Say that again?"

"My computer terminal at the clinic. Someone logged on. I just got the alert."

"What time is it?" He glanced at the table and the glowing red numbers on his bedside clock, which read 10:55. He slipped out of the bedroom and down the hall to the kitchen, one hand pressed to his forehead.

"Hector? Are you there?"

"Are you sure?" he asked.

"Yes, I'm sure!"

"What about the passwords?"

"I don't know how. But someone got in. What do we do?"

He couldn't call the police and report a break-in. That was for sure.

"It's that woman. The detective. I knew that fire alarm was something," said Betty. "I'll bet you she did something to my computer. She might be with the police right now. Oh, Hector. Should we run?"

"No. Easy, Betty. Everything is encrypted. Right?"

"Yes. That's right. No one can see the important information."

He heard her breathing in the phone receiver, fast, panting. He got excited thinking of her there in her house, in her nightgown, alone and scared.

"I'll send Churkin after Detective Yokota. He'll take care of it."

"Well, he hasn't. Has he?"

"Let me make a call. Stay home. Do not go to that clinic. It could be a trap."

"Yes, Hector. But I'm scared."

"You want me to come over?"

AVA MOTIONED HIM into the room.

"My computer is decrypting the files from Mills's computer. She had them password-protected but now that I'm in, it should be fairly simple to unlock what's inside."

"How long will that take?" He glanced at the computer on the glass table.

"It will chime when it's done." She cast him a smile that she hoped let him know what she was thinking.

Ava seemed closer to finding Louisa than ever before. Her younger nieces were safe and Kee was here with her. She felt optimistic for the first time since her arrival.

"Did you call Bear Den?" asked Kee, glancing about the empty living room.

She filled him in. Her sister's smaller girls were all safe and someone from his tribal police was watching this house. Sara was beyond her help at the moment. Perhaps this was the kick in the behind that Sara needed to get serious about recovery. She hoped so. In the meantime, those little ones would need protecting and raising. She just didn't think their grandmother was the right one for the job.

"So we wait for your computer and see what we've got."

She smiled, liking the way he said *we*. It was ironic how her feelings had done such a 180. First she'd tried to find proof of his guilt. Now she just wanted to keep him from getting hurt. No, that wasn't all, she admitted to herself. She wanted more than his safety. But first he'd have to forgive her deceit.

Her smile faltered. "There's no *we*, Kee. I did this. It's all me and if anyone asks you, you have no idea who pulled that fire alarm."

"Did Tinnin ask you?"

"Of course. I denied it and didn't mention you. I won't, either. When this all falls apart, and it will, I want you clear. Your tribe will need you more than ever once I take down Hauser and Mills."

"Do you think anyone here will believe that I didn't know? That I wasn't involved? My innocence will play as stupidity."

She thought he might be right.

"All I know for sure is that I want this solved as badly as you do now. I don't like being used or lied to. And I am sickened by what is happening. It was so hard to see Hauser today and think that he's wearing some kind of a mask. That he could be capable of this. I still have hope that you're wrong. That someone else has done this."

"We should know soon." She could not meet his gaze when next she spoke. "Kee, I'm sorry I didn't see sooner what kind of a man you are. I regret deceiving you."

"It's part of your job. Isn't it?" he asked, his voice tight and controlled.

"It is and usually I'm fine with that. But not this time. You deserved better."

She'd only known him for a week, yet already she was beginning to trust him. It was new ground for Ava. She'd been with men before. But never one she had real feelings for because that would be too dangerous. She'd never wanted to give a man that kind of power. But now she wondered what she had missed by holding back that part of herself.

She could no longer deny that Kee wasn't like other men. He possessed a strong moral compass and seemed genuinely *good*. Growing up, she'd seen time and time again the fallout of loving the wrong man. Look at her own mother's actions. But nothing about Kee screamed *wrong man!*

She offered her hand and he took it, coming in close as he wrapped her up in his arms. She slipped into his arms and pressed against him. Kee's smile changed to something hungry as his lips parted.

"Ava?"

"Kiss me," she said.

His fingers tangled in her hair as he swooped down to take her mouth in a kiss that left her no doubt that he had crossed the point of restraint along with her. They were alone. Safe for the moment, and there was no one she needed to protect or care for.

His tongue thrust with hungry strokes, strong as the rest of him and tempting her with the promise of what he intended to do to her. She wanted it, wanted it all.

The heat and the thrill of his body pressing to hers made her pulse quicken and her breasts ache with need. She lifted one of his hands from her hip to her breast and relished the feel of his fingers splayed and kneading her wanton flesh. The strangled cry that escaped her brought an echoing growl of need from his throat.

He released her to unzip her jacket, pausing at the sight of her shoulder holster. She shucked out of the jacket, removed the holster, blouse and body armor, shoes and slacks, leaving her dressed in only a cotton T-shirt, bra and underwear. He grasped the bottom of her white T-shirt. Their eyes met and the mutual desire sparked as he swept the garment up and over her head. She tugged his shirt from the fitted jeans and slid her hands up his bare back. His skin was warm and taut. The sensitive nerves on the pads of her fingers relayed each curve and hollow as he unbuttoned the cuffs of his shirt and the collar, reaching over his head to grab the back of the cotton shirt and tug it free. It fell upon hers as she reached for his belt. She had it off as he used the heel of one cowboy boot to catch the heel of the other and step free. Then he hopped to that foot to drag off the remaining boot. He lost an inch at the removal of his footwear, which brought her head just under his chin. Perfect for kissing, she decided as his mouth slashed across hers, stoking the fire of need in her belly.

She felt his hand slide over the back of her bra and lifted her hands to the center of her chest to the clasp that held her undergarment. With its release she felt free and unfettered as he stepped back to look at her.

"I'll never forget this sight for as long as I live,"

he said. "Ava, you are the most beautiful woman I have ever seen."

She flushed at the compliment as she devoured the sight of him. His chest was well-defined and his stomach armored with tempting ripples of muscle punctuated by the enticing hollow of his navel. She drew one finger down the center of his chest and watched his nipples bud and his skin turn to goose-flesh. She stopped only when she reached the waist-band of his jeans. The hard, defined ridge made her ache to touch him. She did, rubbing her hand over his erection sheathed in denim.

"I've been thinking about this. Imagining," she said.

His brows lifted. "Me, too."

He stepped closer, his mouth on hers and then on her neck, tasting and nipping. His tongue swirled in delicious circles down the most sensitive spots. When he reached her breast she arched back, giv-ing him access as she leaned against his mouth. The tug and draw sent shards of pleasure through her, stirring a deep, insistent, pulsing need.

He stripped her out of her underwear. She moved only to step clear as she sank to her knees before him. He lowered her to the rug and snatched a couch pillow from the sofa that he tucked under her hips, lifting her and giving him better access to every-thing.

Kee sank between her legs and Ava bit her lower

lip as the sensation built, climbing and cresting until she crashed over the edge of her release.

She cried out and lifted up to meet his mouth and that clever, darting tongue. Oh, how she loved a man who knew his way about. She reached for him, drawing him upward, and he kissed his way back over her hips and stomach and neck.

"That was amazing," she whispered.

He grinned, pleased with himself, and she stroked his cheek as she reached, finding him hard with want.

He was a passionate lover, so different from the careful man. Kee showed her a vulnerability that was completely unexpected. He reached into his front pocket.

She thought back to how she would have reacted only a week ago if he had made such a move. He withdrew a blue foil packet and offered it to her. His caution was only for her, making sure he wore protection before he saw to his needs. Ava tore the packet with her teeth and then reached for the rivet of his jeans.

THE LAPTOP CHIMED a tune and Kee made a sound as he came awake, his arm tightening about her.

"What?" He opened his eyes to the unfamiliar living room. It took a moment to remember where he was.

Ava lay curled beside him on her sister's couch, naked with only the crocheted afghan to cover her hips. One knee was draped over his thigh and her hand tightened on his opposite shoulder as the chime sounded again. How long had they been asleep?

He thought back on their lovemaking. She was so sweet. He had expected passion. Ava was passionate about everything and fierce and hot-blooded. But the sweetness had been an unexpected gift.

She pushed her hair out of her face and smiled up at him, her chin now resting on top of her closed fist. Their eyes met and he saw no regret, just the tousled hair and sleepy face of the woman he thought was very quickly wheedling into his heart.

The chime rang again and Ava stiffened.

"My computer. It's finished decoding." She swept to her seat in a graceful spin that brought the afghan away with her as she crossed the room to the glass dining room table.

Kee reached for his briefs and jeans, slipping into them before following her. She sat clutching the crocheted blanket to her chest as she peered at the glowing laptop. Kee retrieved his phone and saw it was now officially tomorrow. Ten after one on Saturday, one week since he had met Ava. That seemed completely impossible, but it was so.

He tried and failed to ignore the tug of need that pulsed within. He rested a hand on her shoulder and she covered it with hers as she glanced back at him. Their eyes met and he knew he could not handle Ava Hood any more than he could handle this situation. He was in over his head.

He was suddenly afraid of what she would find there. He'd broken the law for her and he knew he'd do whatever she asked. Not just because he needed to know, but because he needed to prove Hector was innocent. Kee was convinced that someone was using his mentor or blackmailing him. Hector just could not have done what Ava thought. He wasn't capable of doing something so very wrong. Once they discovered the truth of his innocence, Ava would look elsewhere for her criminals.

Ava went back to the computer, copying the flash drive onto two other similar ones. Then she began opening documents and spreadsheets rapid-fire as if shooting an automatic weapon.

"Look!" She pointed at the screen and the Excel spreadsheet. "A list of possible candidates. Girls' names, visits, pregnancy test results and pickup dates."

Kee's stomach twisted as his fears crystallized like shards of glass in his stomach.

"Louisa!" Ava exclaimed. "There she is."

So Betty was involved. Kee made the next step alone. Betty could not have managed such a thing without the help of a physician at the minimum. Hector could run a simple test, of course. Like a pregnancy test. As for inseminating "candidates," as Ava called them, yes, Hector was physically capable. And if he followed the law, he would have a female in the room with him. That should have been one of the nurses, but it might have been Betty. It likely was Betty, he decided and frowned.

Kee sank to the seat beside hers, shoulders sagging with the weight of this discovery.

Ava didn't notice him as she continued to read aloud.

"This might be the birth parents but she's just used numbers to identify them. Betty is very organized." Her fingers flashed on the keys, bringing Kee's world apart. "What I don't see is who picked up the girls and where they were taken. But it's enough. I need to call Tinnin and FBI Agent Forrest. I don't want Hauser and Mills to flee before they can make an arrest." She curled her fingers before the keyboard and blew away a breath. "I was right." She lifted her gaze to him and the smile that curled her lips vanished by slow degrees. "Kee? What's wrong?"

Chapter Sixteen

Kee didn't know where to begin. He stood and snatched up his shirt from the floor. He was on the sofa tugging on his socks and boots a moment later.

"Kee, tell me what's happening."

She held the blanket around her shoulders as she came to sit beside him and reached toward him. He leaned away, avoiding her touch.

"You didn't think Hauser did this," she said.

He drew the legs of his jeans down over the boots and stood.

"Of course I didn't. Now I've betrayed the greatest man I ever knew. Or a man I thought I knew. I don't know what to think."

"He's a monster."

"He's the reason I'm not still limping around this rez. I was so unredeemable my own father chose Ty to drive him instead of me. And the Wolf Posse? I didn't make the smart choice and avoid joining the gang. I tried when I was thirteen. They didn't want me. You know who did? Hector Hauser. He believed in me. Now what do I have?"

"I'm sorry, Kee. But he isn't the man you thought he was."

"He's got a wife and three grown daughters."

"And a mistress. Betty and Hector have been having a longtime affair." She hadn't known the woman involved when she first uncovered the messages, but now she knew. Without a doubt.

His shock showed in his flaring nostrils and sharp intake of breath. He recovered, his brow furrowing. "How do you know that?"

She took his hand. He allowed it but it was like holding a store manikin. His body was stiff and unyielding. He did not clasp her hand or meet her gaze. "Nobody is all bad, Kee. Bad guys have some really good reasons for what they do."

"So call Tinnin. Call the FBI. If this is true, we need to stop it now."

AVA SAT IN the squad room of the Turquoise Canyon police station. The FBI had done their best to get Tinnin to agree to extradite Hauser and Mills from the rez to the FBI field office in Tucson. Tinnin had refused. It was up to the tribal council to make such decisions. Only they had the authority to request that a suspect be tried by the federal court system but rarely did so. This was sovereign land. So while the FBI had jurisdiction to investigate crime, they had no right to demand that either suspect be surrendered to them. Hauser might be many things but he was still Apache and Tinnin would not permit Hauser or Mills to lose sovereign rights without the tribal executive council's approval.

So the FBI had set up here, quickly and with shocking efficiency. Tinnin and Bear Den had both looked over the files that she had provided and agreed to enlist the help of the FBI. Arrest warrants were issued and search warrants obtained.

In the wee hours of the night, Hector Hauser and his wife, Beatrice, were taken into custody. Betty Mills was arrested and all three were transported to the tribe's ceremonial grounds and a temporary, mobile detention unit.

The FBI techs were in the health clinic much of the night and obtained legally what Ava had glimpsed illegally. They discovered the name of "a package," which they determined to be the next girl scheduled to disappear. No time or date had been entered in Mills's carefully maintained logs. The victim's name was Heather Cosay. What they did not find was a location for Louisa or the other girls. It seemed Dr. Hauser and Betty Mills's responsibilities ended after the scheduling of the pickup.

Kee had been grim-faced during the night as he watched the man he had respected arrive in handcuffs. Ava had tried to comfort him but Kee's misery was still palpable. She had nodded off in her chair beside Kee when Forrest arrived to wake her. "Where's Kee?" she asked.

"At the clinic delivering a baby," said Forrest.

Forrest wore a gray suit that still had crisp seams down the legs, despite the fact that he'd been working all night. His white shirt had not fared so well but the charcoal-colored tie covered the worst of the wrinkles. He was clearly Native, with deep brown eyes and short black hair. He was fit and muscular, with an angular face that said he worked more than he ate, and seemed to be in his late thirties.

"Hauser has admitted to seeing the girls as needed for neonatal care at the Darabee location."

"Where Kacey Doka was held?"

"Yes. But after the raid, the Russians holding them decided to use a different physician. Compartmentalize in case Hauser was under surveillance."

Ava rolled her lips between her teeth and felt her heart sink. Had it all been for nothing?

"We don't know where Louisa is," said Ava.

"No. I'm sorry. But this information will go a long way in making this case."

She'd given away her career on a gamble for Louisa, and lost.

Ava glanced at the large clock on the wall. It was Saturday morning, just before seven. The clinic was closed.

"Do you think Hauser would take a deal?" she asked.

Forrest rested the knuckles of one hand on the table to her left. "What kind of a deal?"

"He'll call for the pickup for Heather Cosay. The pickup man will not know what girl to expect. I could be that girl. I could be Heather Cosay."

Forrest gave her an assessing look and pursed his lips. "I'm not sure you can look that young."

"With the right clothing, makeup and hairstyle, I could do it."

"Pass for eighteen?"

Ava was nearly twenty-eight. It was a stretch but everyone said she didn't look her age. She still got proofed every time she went into a bar.

"It would be Mills to take that deal. She's the one who arranges transport," said Forrest.

"She turns witness and makes your case," said Ava, "plus we get the missing women back."

Forrest made a sound that more resembled a growl than a laugh. "Or you get killed."

"We don't have a lot of time here."

"You know what you are doing? Because the way Wallace spins it you're a little bit crazy and your sister is in jail, leaving three little girls with no one but their granny to see to them. Have you thought of that? Really thought?"

"There should be four little girls," Ava countered. "Louisa is missing and crazy is exactly what you need right now."

"I'll bring it to my boss. But don't get your hopes up. If we offer up a decoy girl, it will likely be one of our agents."

"You got someone who speaks Tonto Apache? Someone who can pass for nineteen and who can be briefed and ready in…" She glanced at the wall clock. "In three hours?"

Chapter Seventeen

Kee Redhorse had been with Ava most of the night, but a woman in labor had drawn him away so he had not been there in those all-important few minutes when she somehow convinced the Federal Bureau of Investigation to use her as a body double for the woman who was scheduled to be captured next.

He found out upon arrival at the tribal gathering grounds from Detective Bear Den and by then Ava was already gone.

When Bear Den told him what Ava was doing, he'd lost his mind.

Had he actually taken a swing at a detective?

Bear Den had dodged and had him in an armlock, which he held until Kee had stopped cursing in Tonto. Then he'd turned him loose.

Bear Den told him that Ava had been in the clinic and that his sister-in-law Lori had assisted the FBI in taking a photo of Ava at their reception area in the same manner Betty would for any new patient's file. This was important because it was the type of digital image Betty Mills routinely sent to the kidnappers to help them ID their target. They had used Heather Cosay's real photo as a guide for Ava's hair and makeup.

She'd been prepped to take the young woman's place.

"Where is she now?" Kee was so angry it was hard to think, let alone speak.

"You can't go to her."

"Hell I can't."

Kee knew better than to challenge Bear Den.

The wall clock in the squad room read 10:23 a.m. on Saturday morning.

"If she dies, I blame you," said Kee.

"If you move your truck in the next hour, I arrest you," he replied.

His gut told him she was in danger.

"It's our best chance to find them. The missing. If she can convince the Russians that she's Heather, they'll bring her to the others."

"You don't know that!" Kee threw his arms up. "They could take her anywhere. They could kill her on the spot. Ava looks young, but eighteen? And she acts like a cop. We need to stop her."

"She won't be alone," said Bear Den. "Tinnin is already on-site and FBI has surveillance in place. They will know where she is every second."

"I can't stand it if anything happens to her," said Kee.

"I know the feeling." Bear Den blew out a blast of air. Kee had thought he'd told Ava his feelings for her without words on Friday night, but the moment the opportunity to find her niece arose she'd taken the chance.

"She didn't even tell me," he said.

He did not figure into her decisions in the least, so clearly his feelings for her were one-sided.

"There wasn't time."

Kee's snort told Bear Den what he thought of that excuse.

"She's got guts. You have to admire that," said the detective.

Kee said nothing. His hurt and anger were still too raw.

"You care that much," said Bear Den, "makes me wonder why."

Kee shook his head. How did he explain caring for a woman so much it hurt and then having her not even seem to notice you were gone.

"She's worth it, I think," said Bear Den.

"What is?" asked Kee.

"Loving Ava."

Kee stood couldn't speak past the lump in his throat. Kee left him at the station. He heard Bear Den pick up his radio and call for Kee to have an escort. Before Kee reached his old truck there was a squad car behind him. He clenched his jaw until it ached and the burning in his eyes ceased. Then he turned over the motor and waited for his vision to clear. He did not wipe at the tears that rolled down his face as he drove. He parked and flicked off the motor. Then he tugged his shirttails from his trousers and used them to wipe his face.

He drove past his mother's place and noticed that her minivan was missing. Likely his mother, her husband, sister and the three foster girls were still at church. Jake would not be joining them because he'd be working the biggest case since the eco-extremists attack. Colt would not be coming because he was in witness protection. There was one person he could go to who might know what was happening. Whether Ty would tell him about it was another matter. Ty had always kept secrets. Kee just prayed Ty had nothing to do with Heather Cosay.

As he exited the truck, the squad car parked across the road in the turnaround. Halfway to the garage, Hemi trotted out from the cover of the carport to greet Kee. For reasons he did not wish to examine, he dropped to one knee and hugged the dog, burying his face in the thick coat at her neck.

When he lifted his head it was to see that Ty's motorcycle was already there in the carport and his brother was making his way in Kee's direction.

"What's wrong?" Ty asked.

Kee told him. He didn't hold back a thing, even though he knew Ty had connections to the tribe's gang. He trusted Ty and would always trust him, even with Ava's life.

"This is bad," Ty said, giving his head a slow shake from side to side.

Kee's anxiety doubled.

"What is?"

"I didn't know about Day until afterward. But when we found his bike, I went to Faras. He told me they sent someone for Day."

Faras Pike was the head of the tribe's gang. Kee knew him but avoided him when possible. That was something Ty had never been able to do.

"They? Who's they? The Wolf Posse?"

"No. Not our guys. The ones the posse is working with. Moving drugs, mostly. At least that's the part of the organization that I know about. Keeping the cars ready to roll, that's my gig. They're sending him again."

"Who?"

"The same one they sent after Day."

Kee didn't know if this was a trick or a trap. He didn't know what to do.

"Why would Faras tell you?"

"I'm a driver. A good one."

Driver? That's what he'd been doing for their dad when they got caught but Ty had crashed the getaway car.

"You helped the killer get away?"

Ty shook his head. "Didn't need me for Day. No heat."

"Who are they after today?" The answer came to him at the same moment as he finished the question. "No." He was gasping now, trying to get the words past the panic. "They couldn't have known who she was. No one did."

"Someone might have figured it out."

"He's after Heather," said Kee.

"Heather? Heather who?"

"The next surrogate."

Ty laced his fingers behind his neck and paced away and then back. "No. No. No. This is really bad." He gripped Kee hard by both shoulders and gave him a little shake. "They don't send this guy on pickups. You understand?"

"Are they sending him for Ava?"

Ty's look was bereft. "I don't know. But he's here for someone. She's my first guess."

"Why did Faras call you? Why would he even tell you?"

Ty leveled him with a hard stare. "Because I'm the driver assigned to get him off the rez if something goes wrong."

Kee glanced back at the empty street. Yury Churkin was coming for Ava.

"Call him off!" shouted Kee.

"I can't do that. And when they call me it will be too late. She'll be dead."

Kee reached for his phone, dialing Ava as Ty's phone rang. The two brothers stared at one another for an instant before Ty answered the call.

AVA STEPPED OUT of the shower and onto the white terry-cloth bath mat on the pink tiled floor. This house had been built in the 1950s and all the tiles were pink trimmed with black. The sink and tub were also pink. Only the toilet, switched out for a more water-efficient model, was white.

Ava worried that the lack of sleep and resulting puffiness under her eyes would make it difficult for anyone to believe that she was ten years younger than her actual age. She'd said she could do it and she intended to make this work.

Mills had told the FBI that she routinely sent the kidnappers the target's address and the patient photo from the clinic. Mills had helped the FBI send the photo of Ava impersonating Heather to the correct address. Now Ava stared at Heather's real photo, which showed a pretty young face with too much eye makeup, hair in pigtails and a mouth covered in bright pink lipstick. So that was the look Ava would emulate again, just as she did for the photo that would soon be in her kidnapper's hands. Ava would use Heather's photo as a guide to apply her makeup.

Thankfully, they were of similar height, weight and build. The Russian captors never saw the girls until pickup.

She toweled off and headed to the bedroom, where she combed out the tangles, parted and tugged her shoulder-length hair into pigtails. Ava took special care to use the fastenings that included a tracker. She would have trackers on her phone, in her sneakers and in her hair.

After she had her hair arranged, she dressed in Louisa's things. The denim shorts were way too short for her liking, with the pockets sticking out below the frayed hem at each leg. The baby doll T-shirt was thin and showed her skin and the color of her bra right through the fabric.

"How do girls wear this stuff?" she asked her reflection.

Ava applied her makeup and then regarded herself in the full-length mirror affixed to the back of Louisa's bedroom door. A stranger stared back at her with eyes ringed with black eyeliner, glossy pink lips and legs that went on and on until they met the running shoes. She was glad to be wearing shoes in which she could run. She wore no body armor and felt positively naked without her service weapon. Ava shifted from side to side but could not feel the tracker that she had slipped in between the insole and sole of her right shoe.

She glanced at her cell phone. Agent Forrest would call her when contact had been made and the kidnappers were en route. Then she would be transported to Heather's current residence to wait. For now she had nothing to do but prepare. She marked the time on her phone as she wondered if Agent Forrest had succeeded yet in collecting the real Heather and her boyfriend, Lenny.

She knew that Heather lived with her boyfriend, since her father had found out about the boy and had tossed her out a month ago. According to Mills, Heather had been seen at the clinic on Friday for the ruse of anemia, had tested positive for pregnancy and did not yet suspect she was with child. Lenny was also to be taken into custody for his own safety and because he had affiliations with the Wolf Posse.

Mills had confessed that she had notified the

pickup team on Friday that a "package" was ready despite Hauser's worry that there was too much heat. But the Russians were insistent and Mills feared for their safety if she did not comply.

The FBI would receive a text on Mills's prepaid phone sometime today requesting pickup details. Mills had cooperated, describing her normal routine with agents as part of her deal to avoid prosecution, which included texting back an address, photo and any other information such as a car make and model and license if pertinent. Mills had sent this intel on a burner phone provided by their associates. At nine this morning, Ava's photo had been sent. In the image she had worn Louisa's style of makeup as they'd created a photo at the health clinic, where all patient photos were taken and added to the files during intake. This digital image was exactly the sort that Mills would have sent in prior pickups.

Ava was ready.

There was something wrong. She felt a presence now that had been absent before. She cocked her head but heard nothing. But her body tensed. Someone was in the house.

Her mind flew through the possibilities. The FBI would not enter her house unannounced. Kee wouldn't, either.

She hesitated, confused. Was it one of the agents? Had something happened?

"Hello?" she called. "Sylavania? Is that you?"

Ava was halfway across the living room when she

found Woody in the hall before her door. He had been out in the backyard and his appearance meant someone had let him in. A chill ran up her arms.

A man stepped into view. He was big, white, with a balding head and eyes the color of storm clouds. Numerous gang-style tattoos encircled his upper arms marred by long, healing scabs on each forearm. Her eyes widened as she spotted the dagger tattoo at his throat.

Yury Churkin.

She recognized him instantly.

She knew him. But did he know her?

He looked as surprised to see her as she was to see him. He lifted his pistol, pointing it at her gut. Woody left her to greet the new arrival, tail wagging. Yury ignored the canine, focusing on Ava instead.

"What are you doing here?" he asked.

Ava could not have spoken if she tried. Her heart was pounding so fast she could barely hear and all her muscles went tight. Her breath came in rapid pants through her open mouth, bringing the sickly sweet fragrance of bubblegum from the lipstick into her lungs.

He outweighed her by more than a hundred pounds.

Ava backed down the hall and he advanced in slow pursuit.

What was happening? Why was he here?

"What's your name?" he asked.

"H-Heather," she stammered. "Heather Cosay."

He didn't recognize her, then. Not yet anyway.

Her mouth was so dry. Had he come to kill Detective Hood and somehow stumbled on the woman next to be taken? As long as he thought she was Heather, he might not kill her. But the instant they figured out who she really was, she was dead.

"Where's the detective?"

"I don't know. She left a few minutes ago."

"Why are you here?" he asked again, his voice raised as he advanced. Woody trotted along with him, tail wagging. Churkin ignored him.

Ava tried to figure it out, what Churkin would think. If Heather was here in Ava's sister's house, that would mean she knew that Heather was going to be taken. Didn't it?

"She's picking up her nieces. I'm supposed to babysit so she can take her sister to mass."

Churkin spoke in Russian, what she assumed was a curse or a string of them. Would he buy the coincidence? Staying alive was her first priority but it did strike her that she still might be taken to Louisa and as long as she had the trackers, they could follow her.

He advanced. She judged the distance to the bedroom door and found it too far.

"Who are you? What do you want?" she said. The fear was genuine, no reason to act.

He said nothing. She ran and he caught her by one pigtail. It was one of the reasons officers wore their long hair pinned up. Hair made too easy a handle. He dragged her backward. In a moment he had her in a choke hold as one hand ran up her hip and to her backside, where he plucked the phone from her rear pocket.

Ava thrashed as her attacker threw her over a shoulder.

"Let me go."

He was taking her down the hall to the bedroom. Oh, God, was he going to rape her?

Churkin threw her on the bed. She rolled to escape off the other side but he gripped her ankle, dragging her back to the middle of the bed with one hand. The other held her phone, which was now ringing. She knew the ringtone because she'd set it. Kee was phoning.

Her attacker set the ringing phone on the bedside table. Where was his gun? She kicked out at him, missing his face by inches. He growled and tugged her toward him with the ankle he clasped and slapped her across the face with his free hand. Stunned, she fell back to the bed and stared up at the crack that traveled like a staircase across Sara's ceiling.

He flipped one side of the coverlet over her and wrapped her so quickly Ava had little time to grab a breath before she was surrounded by the covering. A fly caught in the spider's web. She had the tracker in her hair and one in her shoe. But there was no surveillance in her sister's house. They had not needed it and had set up only in Heather's residence. How had he gotten past the FBI waiting out front?

Her phone stopped ringing. He lifted her over his shoulder and carried her again. The house phone began to ring. The FBI? She tracked their progress by the sound. Woody's collar jangled as he followed them out of Sara's bedroom and down the hallway runner. Churkin's shoes clicked on the tile and then thudded on the living room carpet and finally gave a soft tapping on the kitchen linoleum. He was going out the rear door and all the agents were out front. Did he know that they were there?

The hot exterior air told her they were in the backyard, but her head was still covered. She could see nothing. Behind her, the door clicked shut. She listened for Woody's collar but heard nothing.

Could anyone see her? Was there anyone in the backyard that ran to the crumpling fence that butted against the neighbor's yard this Sunday morning? Most of Sara's neighbors would be in church or still in bed.

She marked the distance, guessing that they were traveling between the neighbor's homes that sat on the street behind her sister's place. When he dropped her in the trunk, she thought she might have a chance. All trunks in newer-model cars had release levers that glowed in the dark. But then he uncovered her lower legs. A moment later she felt the bite of a plastic zip tie cinched around her ankles. The door closed a moment later and she found herself in total darkness.

She'd known this might happen when she'd given Hauser her name. Known that he could use it to discover who she really was. She'd recognized, too, that her attempts to get Louisa back might bring trouble to her sister and youngest nieces. She'd thought she could protect them. When she realized she couldn't she'd called in help. Her sister and nieces were safe. As she lay there, thinking, half-naked and wrapped like a human burrito in the sweltering trunk of a killer's car, she hoped she'd have the chance to do what she came for and find Louisa.

This was the hired killer they'd sent for Day. Would they send an assassin to capture Heather? This was wrong. All wrong. But some part of her still wanted this to work, to find Louisa and bring her home.

Why hadn't Mills told them that Churkin knew who she was? She could see Betty laughing inside with the knowledge that the killer was stalking Ava, even as she seemed to cooperate. Mills had broken the terms of her plea deal. Of course, Ava would have to survive to tell anyone.

Chapter Eighteen

The fear swept down on Kee like a thundercloud. Inside, the lightning crashed through his nervous system as his mind and body seemed to break apart. Agent Forrest confirmed his fears. Ava was missing from her sister's home.

"I don't understand," said Kee to Agent Forrest. He had the phone on speaker as Ty drove. "She's not at her sister's."

"Looks like she was abducted from this location using the coverlet from her sister's bed," said Forrest.

"But you're following her?" asked Kee.

"Yes. We have a team en route to her location."

"Where?"

"Toward Antelope Lake."

Ty shook his head.

"Keep me updated." Kee hung up. "What does that mean?" he asked Ty.

"First of all, the Russian would have killed Ava on-site the moment he made contact, and he would have left her body there because driving around with a body is dangerous."

"But he didn't do that."

"Which I don't understand. He took her. That makes no sense."

Kee rubbed his hands nervously. "Does Yury pick up the captives?"

"I don't know anything about that. I just know that this Russian is a professional killer. They bring him in when Hauser has trouble."

"He's done this before?"

Ty nodded and mentioned the shooting that had gone unsolved. Kee knew her. Had treated her. Been unable to save her.

"What did she do?"

Ty shrugged. "Overheard something. Stumbled on something or just asked the wrong question to the wrong person. All I know is that she's dead and Faras told me it was 'The Russian.'"

"Would Faras know about the pickup of Heather Cosay?"

"Of course he'd know, but I can't call and ask him. Now can I?"

"I think I know the Russian's name. I saw him. Saw Hauser treat him. The name is Yury Churkin. Big, tatted up with scratches on both forearms."

Ty scowled. "Sounds right."

"Would Churkin know what she looked like?"

"Who, Ava?"

"Yes. Does Churkin have the photo of Ava posing as Heather?"

"Again. It's possible."

"But she's not dead. Yury went to Sara's house to kill Ava and instead he found the young woman he thinks is Heather Cosay. Bear Den told me that the FBI would send Heather's details but would use Ava's photo. Maybe the Russian saw that photo, too."

Ty gaped. "It explains why they didn't find her body."

Kee sat back in the bucket seat. "She's alive. If she convinced him she's Heather, then he would have taken her."

"Even though it's not his job?" asked Ty.

"Maybe. Anyway, it's a theory."

"We need to find the holding facility. FBI will find it. She's being tracked," said Kee.

"Not for long. If, and that is a big *if*, the FBI gets to her before they strip her clean, they have a chance. If the Feds miss her, and they probably will, she'll be in the holding facility."

"Where is that?"

Ty pressed his lips tight and cast Kee an apologetic look.

"You don't know. Do you?" Kee asked.

"Not my area. Cars and transport, remember?" said Ty. "Only reason I know about the girls at all is because of what happened to Jake and then to Colt and Kacey."

He meant their younger brothers. Jake had found a baby born by a woman who'd evaded capture, and Kacey, then pregnant, had escaped capture and run home to the rez and her ex-boyfriend, their little brother Colt.

"I know who does know the holding location," said Ty.

"Who?"

"Hauser. He has to. Kacey said he's the one who preps, checks them and delivers the babies."

"He's locked up in the tribal jail," said Kee.

"Then that's our first stop."

AVA SHIFTED IN the stifling comforter. The blanket and the hot air in the hot trunk smothered her so she stewed in her own sweat. Her skin was slick and her hair wet.

She hoped that the FBI was now tracking her. Enough time had passed for them to have recognized that she was missing and begin the trace. She just had to be patient. She just had to trust...

It wasn't her strongest suit. Trusting. In fact, she could count on one hand the number of people she did trust. And that list unfortunately did not include the FBI. It included one man, Kee Redhorse. But Kee did not have the experience to find her.

As her fear rose up in her throat, it was to Kee that she called out. Kee Redhorse who she summoned. Despite what her rational mind told her, her heart whispered his name.

The vibrations in the car changed. She recognized the difference. They had left the paved road and were now traveling over dirt and gravel. She tried to think of where he might be taking her. The time they traveled and the sound of the tires on the highway helped her calculate the distance and made her believe they were still on the reservation. The Turquoise Canyon reservation climbed up Turquoise Ridge. But there was no way over the ridge that involved a car. And all roads off the reservation ran along the paved highway that followed the river to the east and west.

The car slowed, turned, rolled on and on as sweat poured off her body. She was dizzy from the heat when the car finally pulled to a stop. Dust seeped into the trunk and she gagged, choking. The front door opened and slammed. She heard the trunk latch release. And still she could not breathe until he pulled her, blanket and all, from the trunk. Cool air reached her and she breathed deep. She felt wrung out as a dishrag as he tossed her over his shoulder and carried her a short distance. She could see nothing but the blurry image of the coverlet before her eyes. She knew when he brought her inside because of the change of light. And she felt the hardwood planking as he dropped her to the floor.

She braced to fight, fearing she would lose. Churkin was big, rested and had made the journey in the air-conditioned cab of the car. And fighting was dangerous because, if she lost, he might wonder how a sixteen-year-old girl came to have the hand-to-hand combat experience of an army sergeant.

She just needed to stay alive until the FBI found her. They were coming. They had to be.

What happened next happened so fast she could

barely manage to kick and claw at her attackers. Two men unwrapped her and with shocking speed tore every stitch of clothing from her body.

Churkin said something in Russian to the other man and he stooped to tug the clips and ties from her hair.

No. No. No. The trackers. They'd taken every one of them. Without them, she was lost. As lost as a stone thrown in a lake. She had a good look at the second man as they tossed her a garment. She lifted the offering in one hand and glanced from the drab fabric to Churkin.

"Put on," he ordered.

She did. Sliding her arms into the sleeveless wrap dress and tying the knot of the thin fastenings at her hip. There was no belt. Nothing for her to use as a weapon. Once dressed, she faced the men again.

They were not paying any attention to her. Instead, they spoke in Russian rapidly back and forth. She imagined Churkin was describing the mix-up that had occurred. After all, he'd been sent to eliminate Avangeline Yokota and had instead found the pickup target. She considered the second man. Was he the one assigned to capture Heather Cosay?

Ava cast a quick glance around the cabin. This was clearly some miner's shed. She recognized the rock tailings on the wooden kitchen table. Turquoise Canyon reservation got its name from the ridgeline that was riddled with the veins of precious turquoise. Many of the residents here had claims that were set up in the ridge and were extremely private. The cabin was dusty except for the place where she had been tossed and stripped. Gray blankets covered the two front windows, the sunlight poking through the moth-eaten holes in bright beams.

Churkin and his partner stood between her and the door. But there was the windows as exit and the blankets would protect her from the glass.

Why was it so hot in here? She glanced to the kitchen that consisted of a counter supported by two-by-fours, a sink that likely worked by gravity from a barrel of water on the roof and adjacent to the sink sat a small wood-burning stove on a pad of bricks. Judging from the heat and the red glow visible through the slots in the front grate, the stove was burning, which was odd as the day and the cabin were hot.

Churkin's partner collected her belongings, and used part of her sister's comforter to open the stove. Then he proceeded to feed in one sneaker and then the next. It would be only moments until the trackers were destroyed, she realized.

Ava glanced back to the window, considering. She had wanted Churkin to bring her to the missing women. But now, without the FBI tracking her, it would be doubtful she could escape, let alone rescue the others. In other words, she would be in no better position than the other captives with one very important difference. She was not pregnant. A fact that would become apparent with time.

In other words, she was on her own. She guessed this cabin was likely isolated. The complete confidence of the men told her that screaming would bring no help. But she knew the out-of-doors and she was strong and fast. They had given her no shoes. That would be a handicap. And she might still be injured by glass in the fall. She saw no other choice. She glanced to her captors. One was on one knee before the stove, using a stick to feed her shorts and underwear into the woodstove. Churkin stood with arms folded, watching the proceedings. She surmised he would stay until she was transferred to the custody of the second man. Then perhaps he would go back after his target.

Ava took a deep breath and ran toward the covered window. She jumped, ducking her head and leading with her shoulder, curling her legs up as she struck the blanket and window at once. The blanket enveloped her as the glass exploded outward.

Chapter Nineteen

Kee and Ty met Chief Tinnin at the nearly empty police station at 11:53 a.m. Tinnin told Ty to stay put in the squad room and walked Kee toward the interrogation room.

"This place still looks closed," said Kee.

"Everyone is out looking for Ava. Except Forrest. He's in with Hauser." Tinnin swung along on his crutches and one good leg that did not entirely straighten. Kee knew he'd been a bronc buster in the rodeo. His father had told him that Tinnin had been the best on the rez and had even been on TV at Madison Square Garden. Broken bones hadn't stopped him, but when he'd wrecked his knees he had to give it up.

"You know that Hauser isn't going to give us this for nothing?" said Tinnin.

Kee didn't care. They needed to find Ava.

"Which means I have to offer a deal. Which means that bastard won't do time."

"That can't happen," said Kee.

Tinnin grimaced. "But it might. You leave this to me."

Tinnin stopped outside the interrogation room and paused a long moment. Tinnin raked a hand through his graying hair, letting it rest on the back of his tanned brown neck. "Wait here."

Kee paced up and down the hall outside the interrogation room, pausing at the one-way mirror on occasion. Tinnin sat beside Forrest across from Hauser with no table between them and almost knee to knee as if they were all old friends. What was taking so long?

Finally, Tinnin rose and Kee met him at the door. Twenty precious minutes had passed.

"He's agreed to help." Tinnin leaned heavily on his crutches, taking his weight on his armpits and using a free hand to scrub his knuckles over the stubble on his cheek. "The deal all but guarantees that he'd serve no more than five years in jail and avoid federal charges. I don't like it. But I took it." Kee knew that their tribal court system operated apart from state and federal authority. The tribe rarely requested that the state take over prosecution of one of their tribe. But Kee thought Hauser would be a good exception to their practice.

Tinnin straightened. "Since the raid on the facility in Darabee, the Russians have instigated some precautions. According to Hauser, old procedure was to transport the 'package,' is what he called them." Tinnin's mouth twisted in distaste. "They'd take our children. Some are only fourteen. Anyway, he said they take the captives to the facility where Hauser would do a preliminary exam before 'storage.' Again, his term."

"What do they do now?" asked Kee.

"The girls are transported to a small facility on-site. It's a miner's cabin up on Turquoise Ridge. There they are stripped to eliminate any possible tracking devices and only then are they transported to the new holding facility. Apparently there are two holding facilities on our rez."

"You know their locations?" asked Kee.

"Hauser does. But he says the Russians will kill him for betraying them. He's right about that. They'll get to him in jail or prison. So he wants protection. Forrest is talking to him about relocation. Hauser wants his wife and son along but that might be a problem. His wife doesn't want any part of him now. I was the one who notified her of the charges. She's not coming here to see him and she sure isn't going with him if he gets witness protection because she don't want nothing from him except a divorce."

"How long do they keep a captive in the prep area?" asked Kee.

"Not long. I would suspect less than an hour. The whole point is to move the girl quickly out to the facility but still ensure that she is not being tracked by federal authorities. Hauser thought they were just being paranoid. Turns out they were right."

Agent Luke Forrest emerged from the interrogation room, his face grim.

"I offered the deal," said Forrest. "And I have the address."

AVA LANDED HARD on the uneven ground beneath the cabin window. She kicked and flailed, escaping the wool blanket that had acted as window covering. Then she rolled to her feet. She did not pause as she ran along the cabin wall, clearing the corner as the first gunshot sounded.

Behind her came the sound of two Russians arguing and the bang of the front door crashing.

Ava glanced about, taking in her surroundings. Behind the cabin was a propane tank. The cabin itself was raised and resting on the stumps of several logs in a wooded area. Through the trunks of the trees she could see the rock face and evidence of mining. A weapon, she thought. The shovel. A pick. It was a poor defense against her captors but better than nothing. Her best hope was to evade recapture.

She did not run to the mining site for the same reason, though she wanted to. It was the direction that the Russians would think she had taken. Instead, she scrambled under the cabin and emerged from the front. Two cars were parked side by side. A quick check showed there were keys in neither.

She had run out of options. Her only chance was to run.

Someone shouted from behind her, the words unrecognizable. Russian. She glanced back to see Churkin, meeting his gaze as he ran at her. He did not draw his weapon but relied on his speed, running her down like a cheetah after a gazelle. His tackle was brutal. The landing even more so.

His partner arrived a moment later. He used plastic restraints similar to the ones Ava had used on several suspects. They zip-tied her hands and feet. She was then carried to the second car and dropped into the trunk. Before slamming the door closed, Churkin spit on her. The warm spittle trailed down her face and neck as the car springs sagged and car doors slammed. The engine engaged and she was moving again.

KEE AND TY stood in the squad room waiting for Tinnin to return. He arrived with Agent Forrest. When Tinnin caught sight of Ty, he glowered.

"You better scat, Ty," said Tinnin.

"My brother asked for my help."

"Only reason you're not in custody now is because the tribal council voted to keep you on the rez until your hearing. And you leave this rez and all bets are off."

Kee broke in. "What hearing?"

"Later," said Ty to Kee and then rested a hand on Kee's shoulder. "I'll be around."

Ty's hand slid away and he sauntered toward the door.

"Leave the rez and you're the FBI's problem," warned Tinnin.

It struck Kee as he watched his brother vanish down the hall that Ty had always been there to support them physically. All through the bad times when Kee's legs were uneven and through the three surgeries required to correct the difference. Ty had protected and defended him. But now Ty was in trouble and who was there to help him?

Ty disappeared down the hallway and out of sight. A moment later, Kee heard his motorcycle engine roar.

Kee turned to Tinnin. "What hearing?"

"Can we focus on Ava?" asked the police chief. The holding facility was off the rez in the resort community of Antelope Lake. Easy access for Hauser to see to the girls and already in the direction of Phoenix, where the expecting biological parents would receive their newborn. Whether they knew the circumstances surrounding their surrogates was doubtful, but Kee thought that finding them was the next step after finding the missing women.

"Hauser says this is the first stop. He'll run another pregnancy test and do a general physical. Since the raid on the Darabee house after Kacey Doka's escape, they have someone else for deliveries. Compartmentalized the operation, in other words," said Tinnin.

"This is our last shot at getting Ava or the others," added Forrest. "Hauser's contacts await his check to verify pregnancy and then transport to the final location for holding until delivery. He never sees them after that."

"As soon as they get her secured at Antelope Lake, they're going to give Hauser a call," said

Tinnin. "That's their system. If he doesn't answer they'll know something is up."

Kee's heart sank.

"We could beat them there. Even better, we could intercept them before they reach the facility," said Kee.

"I have an alternative suggestion," said Agent Forrest.

"What?" asked Kee. He was growing more desperate. Ready to try anything that might get Ava back. How could the FBI have allowed her to endanger herself this way?

If he could only see her safe. He had to. Had to tell her…tell her… Oh, no. This was terrible. Kee gasped as the truth struck him like a blacksmith's hammer ringing on an anvil.

"What is it?" asked Tinnin.

"I love her," said Kee.

"Then you best go get her, son," said Tinnin.

"Dr. Hauser has been grooming Kee to take over the facility for years. He handpicked him when he was a boy. According to Hauser, the Russians know of Kee. When he receives the call, he could bring Kee along. With approval, of course. It's possible that they'll allow Kee into the facility."

Kee shook his head. "How about the FBI just charges the facility with automatic weapons?"

Forrest looked at the ground between them. "Because if Hauser is to be believed, none of the girls inside will be taken alive. They do not want witnesses to be able to identify them or their organization. First sign of attack and they shoot the hostages."

"I'll do it," said Kee.

Tinnin gaped. "Do you even know how to shoot a gun?"

Kee's only answer was to lift his chin.

"How are you going to infiltrate a secure facility guarded by Russian muscle?" asked Tinnin.

"I can because Ava's in there. And I'm going to get her out."

Forrest nodded. "Only Hauser gets in. And maybe Kee."

"Hauser is *my* suspect. I'm not letting him out of custody," said Tinnin.

Kee broke out in a cold sweat. He knew that without Hauser, he would not get into that facility and without Tinnin, they couldn't have Hauser. The FBI technically had jurisdiction over all crimes committed on federal lands and tribal lands fell into that broad category. But to Kee's knowledge, the FBI had never taken over an investigation on sovereign land unless invited by tribal authorities.

He glanced from Tinnin to Forrest as the two faced off and Ava's life hung in the balance.

AVA THOUGHT THE setback of having her wrists, now behind her back, secured to her ankles was something from which she could not recover. Her attempt to escape had brought her into a worse spot.

Seeing Louisa while a captive herself was a dismal prospect, especially if Louisa greeted her, as she expected the girl would. It would be a tell that would likely lead to Ava's immediate execution.

She no longer held hopes that the FBI would find her. Possibly they had found the empty cabin and the burned remains of her clothing. But little else. And there would be nothing to use to track her. Unlike much of the outside world, here on the mountain, in Turquoise Canyon Rez, there were no cameras recording license plates and the faces of drivers. There was only one stoplight and that was at tribal headquarters.

Somehow she had avoided serious injury in her leap out the window but had bruised her shoulder on landing. Her main complaint now was her hands and feet, which she could no longer feel, the pins and needles having ceased long ago.

The infuriating part of her capture—well, there were many, but the one that rankled right now—was knowing that she had likely been driven right past the construction site beside the river right under the nose of a tribal police unit parked there.

This trunk was hot but not dangerously so. She thought that was due to the fact that they were traveling so fast and the day was waning. Her attempts to open the latch holding the trunk shut had failed and made her think that the mechanism had been disabled.

She could hear the blinker clicking. The car

slowed and the road beneath her needed repair judging from the number of potholes they crossed.

When the car stopped her heart began to gallop and her skin went clammy. She'd never felt so helpless in her life and that included the times she had been taken away by protective services and all the times she could not wake her mother from her drug-induced slumber on the sofa.

This was worse. Way, way worse. She was prepared to die. But she wasn't prepared for the terror that preceded it.

She went rigid, listening as she heard a noise, a motor that she could not identify. The car rolled slowly forward and the motor sound came again. The car door opened and closed. The driver groaned as if stretching. Then he called something to someone yet unseen. She did not hear a reply but when the trunk popped open there were two men peering down at her. They were white and one had a cigarette clamped between thin, pitiless lips. She tried to memorize those faces, longing for the opportunity to identify them.

They spoke but the only thing she understood was a name pronounced with a thick Russian accent. *Heather Cozzay.* Heather Cosay.

So, her cover was still intact. The new man, the one with the cigarette, dragged her out of the trunk, scraping her thigh over the latch controls. She glanced beyond them to her surroundings.

She saw the ceiling beams some ten feet above

her. And just beyond her captors a motor boat, perhaps sixteen feet, sat upon a trailer. Her first thought was that she was in a two-or three-car garage. The boat might mean she was on one of the reservoirs. There were four large lakes in the dam system between Goodwin Lake and Antelope Lake. She could not tell the time because they were inside, under bare, fluorescent lights.

The driver flipped open a knife and spun her face down, then released her wrists from her ankles and her ankles from each other. Her bare feet struck the side of the trunk so hard she winced.

She staggered as her legs gave way. The man holding her hoisted her up with a grip that spoke of cruelty.

"Stand up, girlie," he ordered.

She did, somehow, not feeling the ground beneath. Her feet were numb from the lost blood supply. She had to look down to see that her feet actually touched the concrete floor beside the car's dusty tire. The driver flanked her and she was quick-marched through a garage and into an entry of a house that was more upscale than Ava expected. As she was tugged through the kitchen, she saw speckled brown granite countertops littered with bags and boxes of junk food and a white farmhouse sink full with dirty dishes. A haze of cigarette smoke hung like a low-pressure front over the counter peninsula. Clearly the help had the week off.

What would Heather say in this situation? the

voice in her head asked as she noted the full ashtray beside an open laptop on the counter before a stool, a series of text messages displayed on the screen.

"Where are you taking me? Who are you?"

They gave no answer as they pulled her through the living room. With the curtains drawn and the lights out, she could see little as they continued down the hall. The stench of cigarette smoke followed them.

She held her terror in check as they stopped before a closed bedroom door. The man with the cigarette released her arm to grasp the combination lock fixed through the latch secured to the door. There was a click and he pulled the lock open and drew it away.

When they pushed her into the room, she lifted her hands over her face, shielding her identity from anyone who might be in the bedroom already.

The door clicked shut behind her and Ava rolled to her seat to look back at the door. On the opposite side the padlock clicked.

"Aunt Ava?"

Ava turned to see Louisa huddled on a bare queen-size mattress on the floor. Louisa's dark hair hung limp around her pale face. Her knees were drawn up to her chest and her feet were bare. She wore the same sort of wrap dress that Ava now wore.

Louisa scrambled over the mattress to grasp her aunt, clinging like a frightened lost child reunited with her mother. Ava held her niece tight. At least she knew that Louisa was alive. Now if she could just get them out of here.

She looked about the room, taking in her surroundings as she scanned for some way to escape, some tool or weapon. There was nothing in the room except the mattress and the overhead light that was on to illuminate the room. The window curtains were drawn and bars had been fixed to the inside of the frames. There was an open door to the left, through which Ava could see a bathroom sink.

Louisa was sobbing now and Ava rocked her, stroking her head and making soft shushing sounds. But the tears bubbled up in Louisa's throat as the sobs shook her. All the horror and isolation erupting in one terrible display as the fear broke loose of all barriers.

"Where are the others?" she asked.

Louisa lifted her head to meet Ava's stare, her eyes red-rimmed and swimming with tears.

"What others?"

CHIEF TINNIN ARRANGED a conference call with the four available members of the tribal council: Hazel Trans, Linda Herrera, Henry Curtis and Executive Director Zach Gill. The women were in favor of letting Hauser take the deal. They wanted all efforts to focus on the recovery of the missing girls and quickly overcame Henry Curtis's objections that Hauser should face judgment. Forrest had his mole and so when the call came in for Hauser to come check the new girl, he took the call and told them that he had broken his hand and so would be coming with a fellow physician, Dr. Kee Redhorse, as driver and assistant.

Kee, Special Agent Forrest, Chief Tinnin and Detective Bear Den all waited around the speakerphone in the silence that followed.

"Dis is your man?" said Alexie, Hauser's contact.

"Yes."

"I call you back. I have to check with Usov."

The line went dead.

"Did he say Usov?" asked Forrest.

Tinnin nodded. "Yes."

"That might be Leonard Usov. He's a…"

Kee interrupted. "Ava mentioned him! Showed me Churkin's photo and said that Churkin works for Leonard Usov. Said he was an…an…" What was that damn word?

"Avtoritet?" asked Forrest.

"Yes."

"We know Churkin works for Usov. Likely this Alexie fellow does, as well. Usov is connected to the Kuznetsov crime family."

"Atlanta," said Kee. He had very good recall. Had to in order to make it through medical school.

Forrest's brows lifted. "Right again."

Kee wished his brother Ty could come with him. But that would bring him off the rez. Ty was playing a very adult version of the game of tag; his brother was safe only if he kept one foot on home base.

The call came at 5:45 p.m. Ava had been missing for seven hours and Kee was losing his mind, bit by tiny bit, as he imagined what they would do to her if they even suspected that she was a police detective. What if Louisa recognized her and, inadvertently, identified her?

Kee waited in the squad room until Chief Tinnin appeared.

"Hauser got the go-ahead to bring the new doctor. But he's only allowed to the newest facility."

"They have more than one?" asked Kee.

"Apparently."

"How many?" asked Kee.

"No idea. Hauser either doesn't know or he's not saying. I think he knows but is trying to keep some bargaining chips. You ask me, he should give us all of them or no deal. But I'm not the one dangling witness protection in front of him."

"Is Ava with all the missing from our tribe?" asked Kee.

Tinnin shrugged and scratched at the hair at his temple. "Waiting on Forrest. He'll have something, I expect. You know I used to think I understood this place. That I was a part of it. But today I just don't understand anymore. How could one of our own, a physician and a man I called a friend for most of my life, do something like this to our children?"

Kee pressed one hand tight against his mouth. He had no answers.

Tinnin continued on. "He gave my boy all his shots. Came to my house in the middle of the night to treat my wife when she had shingles. So what I really want to know is who was that in my house?"

"He fooled us all," said Kee.

"I thought I was a better judge of character than that."

Kee felt that same sense of betrayal. "I always imagined him as the father I would have chosen."

Forrest led Hauser out of the interrogation room. The men turned to watch Hauser being led past the picture windows lining the wall. His head hung as he walked down the hallway in handcuffs en route to his cell.

Kee rose. "I want to speak to him."

Tinnin lifted a brow. "Don't believe anything he tells you."

Kee nodded and rose. For reasons that he knew in his head were not physical, his leg hurt him as he walked down the hallway, as if even the surgery that corrected the length of his legs had been poisoned by this deceit.

Hector was sitting in one of two small cells that punctuated the end of the hallway just beyond the squad room. He remembered seeing Ty in this cell and his father in the one opposite.

"Kee, my boy!" Hector grinned and rose from his seat to stand with his hands in a relaxed grip on the bars. He might have been greeting him at the clinic on any given day. He did not look stressed or remorseful.

Meanwhile, Kee felt like a bag of sand stacked in a wall against a rising flood. The pressure and the sorrow pushed at him from both inside and out until he thought he might give way.

"Dr. Hauser, how could you do this to our children?"

Hauser flexed his fingers. "They aren't children. They're sexually mature women and not the sort of women we need more of. I can assure you."

Kee thought of Louisa, Ava's niece, and Kacey Doka, his youngest brother's new wife. Not the sort… A fire of rage flicked on in his belly, burning away the sourness and the ache until nothing was left but a hard, solid lump of fury.

"How could you?" This time, his outrage rang in his voice.

"For all of us. They're nothing. No one. Gosh, Kee, they can't even speak their own language. Not a single one of them. Did you know that? I didn't pick anyone important. No one like your lovely sister, Abbie. How is she feeling after that stomach flu?"

"No," said Kee. "You don't get to talk about my sister. You don't get to think about her and you certainly don't get to divert the conversation."

"You were always so smart. So much smarter than your brothers. But not smart enough to see. I wanted to tell you so many times. I was so proud of you and so excited to bring you that lab to run blood work. That was Marta Garcia. She brought us all the equipment to run the blood work on-site. Do you know how many lives she will save? And what was the point of her life? To marry that boy she was running around with and have more babies who don't speak Tonto Apache? Who don't contribute to the ongoing lifeblood of our tribe? Her boyfriend was only a quarter Apache, himself. And her, as well. Their children wouldn't even qualify for the tribal roles. Did you think about that?"

Kee's fury began to freeze into something new. Something icy and more dangerous. He saw Hauser as far worse than a man who had committed despicable acts, because he was remorseless. He didn't feel shame or sorrow or pity.

The only emotion Kee could detect was pride. The corners of Hauser's mouth lifted in a pleasant smile.

"You understand?" He released the bars to turn his palms up as if offering a perfectly reasonable argument. "They were contaminants. Just like a pathogen. Removing them for profit was a logical way to strengthen our tribe. Trimming away the deadwood and simultaneously bringing us all the health care we need."

"You sold them."

"Yes!" His voice held elation. "Yes, I did. Precisely. I'm so glad you understand. I've wanted to tell you on so many occasions because you know as well as I do the importance of your work here. We've spoken about it often. And the way you jumped at the chance to stay here with your people. It's so admirable. I couldn't be prouder."

Kee felt sick to his stomach. The salary, the auto stipend and the housing. Which girl's life would pay for all that?

He stared at Hauser as his complete belief in his mentor crumbled like the castle of sand that it had always been.

It was like seeing someone through some diabolical lens. Only he realized this was not a distortion of Hector Hauser. This was the real man, the one that Kee had never actually seen until this moment. But he had been there all along.

"Really. What are we to do?" asked Hauser. "Our population has a life expectancy twenty to thirty years *less* than the non-Native counterparts. And don't tell me that's all because of a bad diet and substandard education. It's the absence of decent health care."

"I don't agree with you. Just to be clear. Selling young women as surrogates… It's reprehensible."

Hauser looked as if Kee had slapped him. His arms slid back inside the cell.

"I thought you would understand. They're nothing. Unimportant. With their futures already determined. It's the tribe that matters. Our Apache culture. We have to survive. I've done all I could think of to make that happen. Educating you. Help-ing the most qualified rise to leadership positions. I've encouraged every single member of our tribe who showed promise, male or female. But this deal I've made with the FBI, it's bad for us. I'll be leav-ing you, my boy." He looked down the hallway. "I hope they don't send me somewhere cold. Or east!" He shivered. "I've never been past the Mississippi, even for medical conferences. Do you think they'll let me continue to practice medicine?"

Kee doubted it, but who could tell.

The man he had idolized was a psychopath, Kee thought. No remorse. No empathy. Just a strong sense of entitlement and self-preservation.

Kee backed away. He had his answers. Dr. Hauser played God. And if Kee were honest with himself, he'd admit that the power to cheat death, the skill to repair broken bodies and the knowledge to heal the sick could mix into a heady cocktail. The com-mand and the respect that he had accepted as his due could lead a man to delusions of greatness. Kee could see it, the small step from mortal to divine. The fact that Kee could see it so clearly frightened him almost as much as Dr. Hauser.

"Tell me when they want me to bring you, Kee. And be assured that I would never give you up. You're like a second son to me. We'll get them back, if that's the price, and I'll be retired like some used-up old racehorse. But you'll be here. I pass my torch to you and you will carry it forward. Won't you, my boy?"

"That's enough, Hector."

Kee startled at the sound of the familiar voice. Chief Tinnin stood in the corridor before the cell, leaning indolently against one of the walls. His timely arrival had prevented Kee from answering. Kee suspected that wasn't accidental. The chief would not want him to say or do anything that might cause Hauser to betray Kee. Expecting his protégé to continue his work was a powerful incentive to see that Kee survived.

He lifted a hand and motioned to Kee. "Time's up."

Kee was happy to exit, relieved in fact. But he did not think he'd ever forget Hauser's twinkling eyes and delighted expression.

"He's insane," whispered Kee to Tinnin.

Tinnin righted his crutches and fell in beside Kee.

"He's not. He knew exactly what he was doing. Granted, he didn't think he'd get caught. But if he's crazy, he can't stand trial."

"If he's in witness protection, he won't be tried, either."

Tinnin's mouth twisted into a snarl. "Hell of a choice. Either I let him go and maybe get our captives back or I lock him up and maybe never see any one of them again. Glad it's not my choice."

"There's another possibility," said Kee.
"What's that?"
"They send us and none of us come back."

Chapter Twenty

The night had passed with Kee getting very little sleep as preparations continued for the rescue and recovery mission. He did not like the word *recovery* because he knew what it meant. Recovery was what you did to a body. It told him exactly how dangerous the FBI considered this mission. He glanced at the clock that showed it was just after 5 a.m. now. He folded his arms across his chest and closed his eyes, trying to rest. Trying to prepare.

Every minute of preparation was another minute that Ava was a captive. When Agent Luke Forrest came to get him just after six, Kee was already wrung out and exhausted.

"We're ready for you," said Forrest.

The operation was explained to him quickly but in great detail. The support force would stay out of sight until Kee made a visual identification of at least one of the girls. Then they would take the house, at which time Kee was to get on the ground and stay there until the house was secure. He was given two pieces of safety equipment, a small communication device that allowed the FBI to hear everything and a small body camera in the bolo that Kee would be wearing as he entered the house.

What they did not give him worried him almost

as much as what they did give him. They did not give him body armor or a weapon.

"Departure in twenty minutes. You have to be ready," said Forrest.

"I will be."

Kee carried the medical bag that had been provided by the FBI for this mission. Hauser would be carrying his usual bag and usual supplies.

His mobile rang and he saw it was Ty. Kee took the call.

"You ready for this?" asked Ty.

"No." Kee did not ask how Ty knew they were preparing an operation or where he was.

"Well, I'd be worried if you were. They give you a weapon?"

"Other than my reflex hammer? No."

"You want one?"

"I'd probably just shoot myself in my bad leg. I'm not a warrior like you, Ty."

"You're not like me. But you *are* a warrior."

Kee loosened the bolo at his throat and then remembered the camera and wondered if it was on. "Ty, I never even completed the warrior training."

While the people of his tribe celebrated the sunrise ceremony for the girls, the boys underwent a rigorous form of physical training, religious education, ceremony and vision quest. Ty had completed all with ease. But Kee, still in a cast, had been able to only watch the physical training that included wrestling and defense tactics. He understood things in principle but he had never spent three days alone in the White Mountains with only a knife, as Ty and the other boys had done. He had been deemed unable to complete the arduous journey from boy to man. And no matter how much education and how many letters he managed to tack on after his name he always felt lacking for this failure.

"You don't learn things just by doing them. You remember how to do a single leg takedown?"

Kee nodded. "In theory."

"You'll do fine. I'll be close."

"What? They're letting you come along?"

KEE HEARD Ty exhale into his phone's receiver, making a sound of pure incredulity. "No. But I'll be there just the same."

"Does Tinnin know?"

Kee looked to the closed door. They'd be coming for him in a moment.

"Don't trust Hauser," his brother insisted.

"I won't."

The knock on the door made Kee jump. He opened the door to find Agent Forrest in the hall. Kee held the phone to his side, Ty still on the other end of the call, he hoped.

"Hauser just received word from the Russians. We now have the address and our teams are moving into position. Kee, we need to go." He turned and walked away.

Kee lifted the phone to his ear. "Gotta go. You'll explain things to Mom? I mean, if it comes to that."

"It won't come to that. Still time to drop out."

He didn't say it with any sort of judgment. But Kee knew the underlying message. Ty did not think he was prepared for this.

"I'm going to get Ava."

AVA SAT WITH Louisa on the single mattress. Beyond the locked door, Ava heard the occasional bang of cupboard doors closing.

"That means they are making our meal." Louisa hugged her knees to her chest and rocked slowly back and forth in a gesture Ava recognized as self-comforting.

Ava judged the time based on the amount of light that came through the closed curtains and bars that barricaded the windows, deciding it was Monday morning. According to Louisa, the guards came twice a day to deliver food. The meals were exceedingly healthy and included pills that Louisa believed to be some sort of One A Day but Ava recognized as neonatal vitamins and iron tablets.

They spoke to them in Russian, which Louisa was beginning to understand. She explained to Ava that they were expected to clean their own bathroom. The towels and their dresses were changed once a week.

The conditions here were much better than the ones described by Kacey Doka. Kacey had spent several months locked in the basement of a house with several other girls sleeping on mattresses with only a thin blanket. Their bathroom facilities had consisted of a toilet and sink.

Louisa now understood how Ava had come to be a fellow captive. She knew that Ava had been mistaken for Heather Cosay and that her survival depended on Louisa making them believe that Ava was Heather. But Ava worried about how long it would take Churkin to report that his target, Ava Hood, had vanished on the same day and at the same time as they had taken Heather. If they put the pieces together before the FBI found her, Ava knew what would happen.

She thought about Kee and wondered if he had missed her yet. She thought of all the things she should have said to him and regretted the time she had kept him in the dark. She had not known him then. But now she did and all regrets centered around Kee Redhorse. Things she would do differently and things she'd never said. Most of all she thought of the time with him that she'd squandered.

"How long until they find us, Heather?" asked Louisa.

She had her fingers in her mouth again after already tearing her cuticles to bloody ribbons. Each fingernail was a short, blunt ragged stub. Ava laid a hand on Louisa's wrist and Louisa dropped her arms back to her knees, slowly returning to the less harmful rocking.

In the time they had been locked together here, Louisa had told Ava some disturbing things about Sara. According to Louisa, Sara drank much more and much more often than even Ava had suspected. Louisa had been driving the family car since she was thirteen because her mother was often too drunk to do so. All of this information only made Ava more determined to survive this situation. Her nieces needed her, far more than she had suspected.

Her first indication that something different was happening was when the voices switched to English. Louisa tensed.

"That's the doctor," said Louisa.

"What doctor?"

"Dr. Hauser. He's been here already to check me. He must be here to check you. Aunt Ava, he'll know. They check your urine. He'll know that you're not pregnant." Louisa was clutching Ava's arm and tugging at her as if in an attempt to flee or hide.

Neither was possible. If this were Dr. Hauser, he would recognize Ava instantly. Ava watched the door, knowing that when it opened her life would end.

Her heart accelerated, beating in a useless staccato in her chest. Her ears buzzed and her skin tingled. Blood pumped, readying her muscles to fight. Time seemed to stretch out to eternity as footfalls in the hall grew nearer and nearer. The key slipped into the lock and the tumblers turned with a deafening clack. She heard the combination lock's dial spin and the bolt release. A moment later the door opened and in stepped Alexie, one of her two captors. He moved aside and she saw the man behind him, expecting either her second captor, Stenka, or Dr. Hauser. Instead she blinked in amazement, meeting the gaze of Dr. Kee Redhorse.

KEE READ THE shock in Ava's expression. Did she think she was betrayed? He stared at her big beautiful dark eyes as relief flooded him and he prayed she would not blow his cover. Her mouth dropped open and then snapped shut. Her eyes flicked from him to Dr. Hauser standing at his side.

On arrival, Hauser had introduced Kee to Alexie and Stenka. The men had given him the once-over and checked his bag but they had not frisked him as the FBI had anticipated. Once Stenka handed over his bag, Kee looped the strap over one shoulder and across his chest. Then Alexie had escorted them down the hall that Kee assumed led to the bedrooms. Kee followed and Hauser trailed behind. He glanced back, wondering if Hauser would run or give him up. But he had just cast Kee a wide, pleasant smile and continued along.

Kee didn't understand it. They had lost sight of their backup. Hauser had a very good chance of escaping. Why didn't he take it? Was his deal for relocation really a better option?

Alexie had opened the door and preceded them

inside. He now stood with one hand upon his Taser, facing Louisa and Ava.

"They don't use weapons around the girls," said Hauser. "Too much chance of harming the fetus."

Kee nodded his understanding; he thought the charge of a Taser would certainly not be good for a fetus.

How far behind them were the agents? They had had a problem, one that he did not know if the agents had anticipated. The house where he and Hector had met Alexie, and where the FBI might have expected to find the missing girls, had been only their first stop. Kee and Hauser had then been rapidly transported through the house to the dock behind it, loaded into a speedboat and jetted to the opposite side of Antelope Lake back toward Red Rock Dam and below the Turquoise Canyon reservation land. There Kee and Hauser left the boat to be escorted up the dock to a lake house. In other words, he thought he was on his own.

All the men paused inside the living area that faced the lake. Their escorts watched the water, Kee suspected, for signs of pursuit.

"So," said Hauser, lifting his splinted hand that was supposed to be broken. "We'll just check the one today, I think."

With that he turned and walked toward the hall. At Kee's hesitation, Alexie pointed after Hauser.

"Exam room is there." His accent made the word

is sound like he said, "ez." He motioned Kee away. "I bring her."

Hauser stepped into the room across the hall. Kee followed, glancing around. In the center of the room sat the short exam table complete with stirrups. The only other piece of furniture was a card table upon which lay the normal equipment used for a pelvic exam, set out on a white towel. Not sterile, Kee decided. It didn't matter, because he was not going to be performing an exam on Ava and neither was Hauser. Kee looked at the medical equipment again with a new eye as he searched for a weapon. If it came to a fight, which side would his mentor choose?

Alexie appeared a moment later, hustling Ava along by the upper arm. Her hands were now fixed before her with a half-inch-thick white zip tie. He did not wait for Ava to climb onto the table but hoisted her up. She scanned the room, taking in her surroundings in a glance. Then she met his gaze and lifted a brow.

"So, give her the check out." His thick Russian accent turned the word *give* into *geeve* and made his *k*'s hard. He probably meant checkup or examination but Kee did not ask for clarification. Alexie left Ava, passing Kee and then coming to a stop just behind him. He folded his arms and glared.

Kee hesitated. Was Alexie going to remain right there, blocking the doorway, standing between them and the hallway?

Where was the FBI? Wherever their staging area, as they had called it, he was afraid it was on the opposite side of the lake. Plus anyone coming by boat would be easily spotted by the second man in the living area. From his position at the kitchen counter, the guard could see both the front and back entrances to the lake house.

The FBI had given him one weapon: pepper spray.

He was out of time. But there was no sound of the front door collapsing or a shout of warning from the kitchen.

Kee looked to Ava and noted that her fingers curled around one of the stirrups, gripping it with white knuckles in both bound hands. Kee stepped between her and Alexie and rummaged in his bag as he retrieved the pepper spray.

Hauser was speaking to Alexie. "I'm going to need a place to wash my hands. I also need rubbing alcohol, which I do not see here."

From somewhere beyond the house, Kee heard a familiar roar and recognized the sound of a Harley Davidson motorcycle.

Stenka shouted from the kitchen.

"There is a motorcycle guy in the drive. Looks Indian."

Ty, thought Kee. His brother had found them before the FBI. It was backup.

Alexie turned toward the hall, reaching for his gun. "Go check it out."

Kee lifted the pepper spray bottle in his sweating hand and pointed it at Alexie. But at that moment the Russian turned and his hand shot out, slapping the aerosol from Kee.

Alexie drew his pistol with surprising speed.

"No!" shouted Hauser.

Hauser lifted both hands and stepped between Kee and Alexie as the latter fired. Hauser doubled over, clutching his middle.

Something in Kee's mind snapped. He stopped thinking and acted. The Russian outweighed him by at least fifty pounds but when Alexie aimed, Kee sidestepped, grasped his wrist and directed the second bullet down to the hardwood flooring. Then he ducked and pivoted, performing the moves he had watched each young man practice again and again in the training he had never been able to complete. Ty had been right. He knew these moves and how to do them. An instant later, Kee had Alexie's hand behind his back and pulled until he heard the cartilage crunch and the joint pop. Alexie's shout of pain was punctuated by the clatter of his pistol striking the ground.

Ava was off the table in the blink of an eye and struck the goon a hard blow to the back of the head. This caused him to roar as he leaped to his feet, shoving Ava so hard into the examination table that both Ava and the table skittered backward, impacting the wall beneath the barred window.

From the outer room came the crash of a window shattering and then the pop of gunfire.

The Russian took a step toward Ava, reaching to retrieve his gun. This time Kee dropped to one strong leg and swept the other from his opponent's back to front, striking him just behind the knees. The mobster's legs buckled and he fell on his back.

Ava recovered Alexie's weapon and shot the Russian three times in the chest. Then she was out the door and struggling with the combination lock that imprisoned Louisa across the hall. Another shot broke the lock open. But the door remained bolted. Kee turned to Hauser, finding dark blood welling between the fingers he clutched to his abdomen.

He looped an arm around Hauser and tried to drag him to his feet. Hauser's eyes popped open.

"No, no. Leave me be. Send help if you can."

Kee lowered him back to his seat and nodded solemnly. "I will."

Hauser smiled and a bright red line of viscous blood dripped from his lips down his chin.

"Proud of you, son."

Kee knew there was nothing in his bag that would stop internal hemorrhage.

He followed Ava as Alexie sat up and shook his head. Kee ran for the door just as his attacker came to his feet. Kee got the door closed an instant before the gangster collided with the solid wooden panel. The vibrations of the impact traveled from Kee's fingertips to his chest. Ava threw the deadbolt, trapping the Russian inside with Hauser. It was only a moment before the pounding began.

"You shot him," said Kee.

"Body armor," she said. "That door won't hold." She raised the pistol and aimed at the door.

"Kee!" The shout came from the kitchen.

He recognized Ty's voice.

"Down here!"

Ty rounded the corner, his opposite hand on his bleeding shoulder. He skidded to a halt, facing Ava's raised pistol.

Chapter Twenty-One

Kee stepped between them, hand raised to Ava.

"How many?" asked Ty.

"One," answered Ava. "In there." She motioned with her head and kept her gun raised. "The other?"

"Down. Kitchen," said Ty.

"His gun?" she asked.

"Threw it out the window."

"Are you armed," she asked.

"I don't carry guns," said Ty.

Ava kept the pistol before her and ready as Alexie thudded against the door beside her.

"Louisa," said Kee. Without thought he bent his knee, lifted his leg, the leg that he had favored since well before the multiple surgeries evened his limbs, and, with all his might, kicked the door imprisoning Louisa.

"No," shouted Ty. But as the screws holding the latch gave way and the wood frame splintered, his objections died. The latch pulled away from its anchors and the door crashed inward.

Kee glanced back at Ty to see him blinking back at him with his mouth gaping.

Ava reached her hand to Louisa. "Come!"

They ran toward the center of the house. Another crash sounded behind the opposite bedroom door.

Kee knew that Alexie would break the solid wooden frame eventually.

Ava and Louisa raced past Ty and toward the kitchen. But Ty called to them.

"Boat! It can hold us all."

"Keys?" asked Ava.

"Not sure."

Ava turned toward the back of the house, dragging Louisa out of sight.

Kee heard a door slide on its track as he cleared the hall and raced past Ty. He glanced toward the kitchen. Stenka lay, facedown and motionless, amid the shards of glass that littered the kitchen floor. Beside him sat the remains of a large terra-cotta pot in jagged ruin surrounded by the dirt, rock and ejected cactus. Ava ducked down beside the living room wall and fired, pinning Alexie as the others raced toward the boat. Alexie returned fire and Ava continued the exchange until the clip emptied. Then she followed the retreating group.

Kee thundered across the deck after Louisa, his medical bag thumping against his side with each stride. By the time he reached the stairs, Louisa had reached the dock that stretched out over the placid blue lake water toward the boat. Ava appeared on the stairs. He ushered her past him and then followed. Ty, already in the boat, spotted the all-important detail, ignition key on a floating keychain in the ignition.

"Keys!" he called back over his shoulder.

Ava ordered Louisa into the boat, shouting instructions as she released the bowline. Kee darted down the stairs to the lake and onto the dock, where he released the stern line as Ty hopped into the captain's seat. It was a small, single outboard engine boat of perhaps twenty feet in length, painted white with blue trim. The four seats bisected the center of the compartment and were situated back-to-back, with the rear seats facing the engine. Louisa sat on the floor, pressed against the far side of the fiberglass hull, both arms outstretched and braced against the empty seat before her.

Ava jumped onto the bow, scrambled over the windshield and into the seat beside Ty at the same time Kee jumped into the boat next to Louisa.

"You're bleeding," said Ava to Ty. "Let me drive."

"You know how?" he asked as he turned over the engine.

"Yes."

He stepped back, switching places, and plunked down in the empty front seat vacated by Ava.

Kee took in the amount of blood soaking Ty's shirt, really seeing it for the first time. Ty's shirt was torn and he held his hand pressed to his shoulder.

"What happened?" asked Kee.

Ava engaged the throttle and they rocketed away from the deck.

"Cut my shoulder on the glass coming through the window."

"Didn't you throw the cactus first?" Kee had to shout to be heard over the engine.

"Happened when I hit the floor. Rolled on it? Don't know." He glanced back the way they had come. Ty pointed. "Gun!"

Kee looked but Ava did not. Instead she turned the wheel sharply, tossing both Kee and Ty to the deck. If either had been standing, they'd be swimming right now.

Louisa closed her eyes and held tight. Kee could not hear the gunfire. But he saw something spark off the engine and spotted the hole in the stern where a bullet had torn through the fiberglass hull.

Ava swerved again, tossing them in the opposite direction as they put distance between them and their attacker. Only when they were at the opposite shore and speeding back down the long narrow lake did Kee lift his head. He could see a man on a dock, Alexie, far away and growing smaller. He watched him turn back toward the house and raise his arm, pointing the pistol. The last thing Kee saw was the FBI swarming down the dock as the Russian's body jerked and fell backward into the lake.

Kee turned to his kit, retrieving scissors to cut away the sleeve of Ty's shirt and get a look at the gash. It was six inches long, jagged and shallow, the bleeding coming from injured capillaries.

Ava straightened her course and shouted back for a phone. Ty slipped one from his pocket, unlocked it and turned it over.

Kee cleaned the laceration under the silent, watchful stare of Louisa. He used Steri-Strips to close the wound. He had the gauze pads in place and was winding an Ace bandage in a figure eight around Ty's shoulder and chest to keep his handiwork in place when it hit him.

"We wouldn't have made it without you," said Kee to his brother.

Ty smiled.

"How did you find us?" Kee asked.

Ty's smile turned grim. "FBI has their sources. I have mine."

"What did it cost you?" said Kee. The Wolf Posse did not give away information for free. He knew that much.

Ty shrugged and then flinched. "A little more than it cost to get Jake his baby."

Kee blinked in shock. He'd helped Jake and Colt and now Kee. And it had cost him. Just what exactly, Kee didn't know.

"Faras?" asked Kee. He knew the head of the Wolf Posse well, as they had been classmates. Two sides of the same coin. Kee had been smart and physically weak. Faras had been smart and athletic. Faras had been recruited. They had not wanted Kee. He'd been angry about it at the time because he never got the free sneakers or money that they'd given Faras.

Ty nodded. "Faras wants me back."

"You weren't back before?" asked Kee.

Ty gave a shake of his head. "Just fixed the cars. Then, after Jake, I had to agree to drive the Russian, if he needed me. Which he didn't. Now..."

Kee's heart sank. It wasn't fair. Ty was a good man. But once you were in the Wolf Posse, it was almost impossible to get out.

Kee's being looked over had been a blessing.

Ava called from the front of the boat. "Does he need medical treatment?"

They answered simultaneously and oppositely.

"Yes," said Kee.

"No," said Ty.

Ava called back. "Forrest wants me to put in at the marina at the north end."

Kee saw the panic on Ty's face. He had not been afraid to throw himself through a plate-glass window or shoot a Russian mobster but the idea of facing Forrest drained the color from his face.

And then Kee remembered Forrest's promise to arrest Ty and charge him with kidnapping if he set foot off the reservation.

"South end!" shouted Kee.

"What?"

"We have to get as close as we can to Red Rock Dam." He moved to stand beside her as she looked up at him.

"Why?"

"It's only a few miles from my reservation. Just up past the dam and it's our sovereign land."

Ava's eyes widened and she glanced back at Ty,

his shirt torn and his shoulder bandaged. Then her attention shifted to Louisa, who huddled on the floor of the boat, knees clutched to her chest with a glazed expression like a combat veteran.

"I'll see to Louisa. But you have to get Ty away from Forrest."

Ava hesitated, hands tight on the steering wheel, the phone pressed between her left hand and the wheel.

"Ava, please."

She turned the wheel.

"I'll tell Forrest where we were and that Hauser is shot."

"They're already there. I saw them shoot Alexie."

Ava set her jaw. "That means they will see us go by."

They buzzed over the water and past the house where they had kept Louisa and Ava, where several agents stood on the dock.

Ava lifted the phone.

"Yes, that's us." She lifted the phone and spoke to Kee. "We've been spotted going the wrong way." Then she spoke back into the phone. "All right. Yes. Just got turned around. Heading back." She disconnected and tossed the phone on the seat beside her as she continued on.

Ty sat in the seat nearest Louisa. The phone winked on with an unknown number. Kee was certain it was Forrest but neither he nor Ava moved to pick it up.

It was twenty long minutes before they reached the river that led to the dam. The force of the water made maneuvering more difficult, but Ava still managed another mile. Kee had rummaged in the boat storage and found a fishing knife and first-aid kit but no water.

They put in on the eastern end of the lake, which was still some thirty miles through rough wooded territory to the rez. There were no roads on that side of the river until you reached their reservation. That might play in Ty's favor.

"See you for supper at Ma's," said Ty.

Kee hugged him on his good side. "Thank you for everything."

Ty removed his boots and went over the side and sloshed through the water to the shore, carrying his boots in one hand. Ava put them in reverse and then turned them back on course. Kee watched his brother climb the bank. He was heading toward the woods when he lost sight of him.

"Think he'll make it?" he asked Ava.

Her reply was a baleful look. She did not. But then, she did not know his brother.

Chapter Twenty-Two

Ava's return to the reservation was less triumphant than she'd imagined. Louisa had been transported to Darabee Hospital, where she was recovering from dehydration, the trauma of her captivity and the discovery that she was pregnant. Ava had left Louisa only to call to check on Olivia, Margarita and Alexandra, who were staying with Chief Tinnin's family for their protection and until other arrangements could be made. Sara was still in tribal jail after her DUI, and chances of her being released did not look good. Fortunately, Chief Tinnin's wife was a lovely woman who had raised up one son and had one left at home. This boy, now sixteen, had apparently come in contact with the woman who had made initial scouting missions to the dam above their reservation for the eco-extremists prior to the attack. His description of the woman had helped bring her to justice.

Dr. Hauser had not survived the gunshot wound to his abdomen and had gotten off easily, in Ava's mind. Betty Mills had broken her plea deal by failing to reveal that Yury Churkin had been sent to kill Ava and so would stand trial. Chief Tinnin believed it highly likely that the tribal council would turn her over to federal authorities.

Yury Churkin had not been apprehended and Ty

Redhorse had not returned to the rez. Because Churkin was still at large, Ava had round-the-clock protection from either Officer Jake Redhorse, Officer Dan Wetselline or Sergeant Harold Shay.

Most troubling of all were the missing. Ava had thought that all the Turquoise Reservation kidnap victims would be in one facility. But Marta Garcia, Brenda Espinoza and Maggie Kesselman were still among the missing.

That troubled her far more than the voice mail message from her boss telling her that she needed to report to Human Resources for her severance interview.

There had been no word on Ty from anyone. She had reported everything that had happened and both the tribal police and the FBI were searching for Ty Redhorse. It was a footrace with both sides competing for the rabbit. She hoped he made it home because federal prison did not seem a just reward for Ty's efforts to rescue his brother. On the kidnapping charge, she had limited information but reserved judgment against him.

Kee had not spoken to her since her return to tribal police a few days ago.

Ava reported to Chief Tinnin at 9 a.m. on Wednesday morning, as he requested. She expected to be escorted off the reservation but she was not going anywhere as long as her nieces were destined for foster care. She had not come here to assume her sister's place as mother to her children, but it was clear someone needed to do so and she was the logical choice. Ava still held hopes that Sara's current situation would bring her to her senses. Her sister's grief at her husband's passing had changed her.

Ava walked the now-familiar route through the tribal headquarters to the police station. She was greeted by Carol Dorset. The veteran dispatcher for the tribe was rubbing lotion into an arthritic knuckle on her index finger. Her hair was pulled back in a simple clip and her lipstick today was a frosted pink.

She smiled brightly, showing the sort of even rows of teeth never created by nature. "He's expecting you."

Ava showed herself across the squad room, past Officer Wetselline, who was on the phone but nodded as she headed by.

Tinnin had the phone cradled between his chin and shoulder, and was absently spinning the rowel of his spur with one hand as he listened to the caller. When he spotted her, he lowered the spur to the desk and then waved her in. She took one of the battered wooden chairs before his cluttered desk.

"All right. Yes, ma'am. I'll send someone out." He returned the handset to the cradle and called to Wetselline. "Go check on Mrs. Alba out on Dustin Road. Her daughter, down in Tucson, can't reach her on the phone."

Wetselline, now on the computer, gave a two-finger salute and headed out.

Tinnin turned his attention on her.

"How is Louisa?"

"She's talking now and she's seen a counselor. I think she'll be all right in time."

"That's good news." Tinnin used his index finger to push the spur to a spot just under the desk lamp. "I heard from Agent Forrest regarding Yury Churkin. They picked him up in Flagstaff. He's in federal custody."

"Great news," she said.

"Yeah. I asked for notification if they get a match between his DNA and the sample from Day's body." Tinnin met her gaze. "That also means you don't need tribal protection any longer."

"Also good news."

The chief tapped his fingers on his desk.

"Anything else?" she asked.

"I hear you got fired."

She nodded slowly. Tinnin had many good qualities, but like many law enforcement officers, tact was not one of them.

"Yes. I'll be heading down to my rez to turn in my badge and gear just as soon as I can."

"So you're a trained police officer who made detective and who will not be getting a glowing reference from your former employer."

"That's about it."

"Well, I wouldn't put you in a squad car, either. Too much chance of getting sued."

She sat back, arms folded. She didn't need to hear

she'd screwed up. She knew it and in her mind it was worth the price. She'd do it again.

"Not sorry, are you?"

"Not a bit."

Tinnin's mouth quirked. "Well, such decisions carry a price. Glad to see you're willing to pay it. I do hate a whiner. So, to the reason I asked you to come in. You see that woman out there?" He lifted his chin toward the dispatch station.

Ava spun and looked at Carol Dorset, headset in place, speaking on the phone to a caller.

"Yes."

"They built this building around her. Carol came in when they added a telephone up here. She was the dispatcher when we didn't even have a title for that job. Her father was our first officer back in the 1920s. Worked under the State Parks Department and he hired me in 1978. Anyway, she's closer to eighty than seventy and she says she just can't sit for eight hours anymore. She's fixing to up and leave me, just like that, after only fifty-three years."

He had her attention.

"So it seems to me that you are overqualified for dispatch but unlikely to get anything better. Also, you might be feeling the need to be here for your nieces. Now, my wife is a good woman, but that three-year-old is likely to kill her."

Ava smiled. Olivia was a challenge.

"Might be able to convince her to babysit after school until you get home from work, though."

"Olivia isn't old enough for school yet."

"But she's getting older every day. Two years will go by just like that." He snapped his fingers. "And as my sons are not likely to bring us grandchildren for a few years. Or, they had better not. My wife needs a project. Olivia is all that." The next part he said under his breath. "Might just keep her from dragging home another stray dog. We have five now and they shed all over everything."

Ava laughed. The girls would love dogs.

"So what do you say?"

"What's the pay?"

He told her and she was glad she was sitting down. "I'd need a raise."

"I'll speak to the tribal council. Might want to join the volunteer fire department, too. They get called on some of our cases."

"You're trying to get a detective at a dispatch salary?"

Tinnin smiled. "I see you will not disappoint me. So, will you take it?"

She thought of Kee and frowned. Seeing him would be painful.

"What's the holdup?" asked Tinnin.

"I'm not sure Kee Redhorse would like me here permanently."

"Why's that?"

"He hasn't been to see me since we were interviewed by the FBI."

Tinnin sat back in his chair and stared, his head

cocked to one side. "And you take that as a sign of disinterest. That about it?"

"Yes, sir."

"Well, let me enlighten you. Kee Redhorse is now the only trained physician on the reservation since that shit Hauser has been fitted for a pine box. Don't expect many mourners at the funeral. Feel sorry for the widow. Always do." ·

Ava drew him back on point. "Kee Redhorse?"

"Oh, yeah. Kee. He's been working twenty-four seven at the clinic. Delivering babies at three in the morning. Treating falls and sickness and everything in between. I heard from Jake that he fell asleep in a birthing room and they had to wake him up for that motor vehicle accident with multiple vics. Long story short, your boy hasn't had time to take a piss, let alone see his girl. And you are his girl, aren't you?"

Ava pressed her hands to her face. She should have known. Even if Kee did plan to never see her again, he would certainly have told her face-to-face. He was just that kind of man. The sort that did things the right way and gave everything and everyone his best. He was the man she knew she could rely on to help her and support her decisions, but she just didn't know if his feelings for her tipped all the way to love. She didn't know which frightened her more: discovering he would have nothing to do with her or discovering that she had misread the situation. There was still hope. Hope that her love might be shared and there was still the possibility that he would tell her that he did not want what she wanted…to spend the rest of her life loving him.

"I've seen you in action," said Tinnin. "So don't you try and convince me you don't have the spine to go and tell that boy you love him."

She lowered her hands and met his intent stare.

"Is it that obvious?"

"To one who has been there, it sure is. I carried my wife's engagement ring around with me for two months."

"How did you get the courage to finally ask her?"

He flushed. "Let's just say she frisked me and found the box."

Ava laughed. He rose and she got to her feet, too.

"So you got a job. You got your sister's house for the foreseeable future. Seems like only one thing's missing." He motioned toward the door. "Go get him."

Chapter Twenty-Three

Kee dragged himself home at midnight Wednesday night, after another sixteen-hour day. He had still not heard from Ty and that troubled him. If the FBI had him, Tinnin would have been notified and Kee had asked the chief to let him know if he heard anything. The chief had word out to the force to look for him and he knew that his brother Jake had left the reservation land to search for him using Hemi, Ty's dog. What did Hemi think, tracking her master?

Jake said it was as if Ty had disappeared and that meant federal custody to Kee.

The house was quiet and he was greeted by only his mother's tabby cat upon entrance. The feline sat in the dark, green eyes glowing and tail wrapped around her front feet. She rose and sauntered out the door without a backward glance. Kee locked up behind her. In the bathroom, he found an explosion of makeup and hair things as the Doka girls continued to expand their territory. He felt like a stranger in his childhood home. He showered with pink soap and shampoo from a pink bottle containing shea butter and coconut. He had to keep one hand on the tile wall in the shower to keep from swaying with fatigue and when he left the bath, with a towel wrapped around his middle, he was followed by the fragrance of coconut. He barely remembered hitting the sofa and woke to the sounds of his mother in the kitchen and the loud, somewhat frantic conversations of the Doka girls preparing to make the bus.

"Long walk," said his mother. She'd made the same threat to each of them, and Colt, Jake and Ty had missed the bus on more than one occasion, discovering their mom did not make idle threats. Abbie had never missed, and he had not, either. He very much doubted that his mother would let young girls walk to school after the disappearances. Things had changed here, and not for the better.

He rolled to his back. Had there been signs that he had missed? Had he been so tied up in his residency and with treating his patients that he had let this happen right under his nose?

His mother appeared in the doorway. "Clinic called."

Kee threw his arm across his eyes and groaned. They didn't officially open for three hours but there had to be something up.

"Auto accident?" he guessed.

"Baby coming," said his mother. "Not urgent but hurry up anyways. Lori is holding down the fort until you get there."

Kee retrieved his phone and saw a missed call from the clinic and no messages.

"Coffee?" asked his mother.

Kee swung his feet to the carpet and nodded. "Do I have time for breakfast?"

"Depends on that baby, I suppose." She reversed course and returned with a piping hot piece of fry bread sprinkled with cinnamon and sugar and his coffee. "Don't even tell me that my fry bread is unhealthy. You're losing weight again. So eat."

He did. When he finished he found the cat staring at him again. She looked disappointed.

"Maybe you should call Ava," he said to himself.

He grabbed his phone and truck keys, then kissed his mother's cheek before heading out.

When he reached the women's health center he checked their one patient who was in active labor. He was there in time to see the baby boy come into the world and sign the paperwork, but his sister-in-law didn't really need his help. She really needed to finish her midwife training. She was so good at this.

When he left the delivery room it was to find Ava waiting in the hall.

"Ava! I was just thinking about you."

Her smile was crooked and only on half her mouth. "Likewise."

"Ah, come on into the break room." He led the way. With each step he grew more and more nervous because he knew he had to tell her. He had to tell the woman who had told him she preferred her solitude and valued her privacy that he wanted her to give up both for him.

Once inside the break room, Kee found

self breathing fast. Judging from the dizziness, he thought his blood pressure was spiking.

"So, how are you?" he asked by way of a clumsy icebreaker.

"Fired." She explained about losing her position and how Louisa was doing and that her sister was now locked up. He'd heard about her sister. It was a one-car accident, thank goodness.

"I'm sorry about your sister."

"Me, too. I'm taking the girls."

His heart sunk. "Taking them where?" He couldn't leave the clinic now. Not with Dr. Hauser's death. It would take time to bring another professional here, especially with the scandal hanging over them.

"Oh, I mean I'm taking custody of them."

He blew away a long breath and nodded, hands on hips. "I think that's a good call. You can be the stability they have lacked. And I know you love them like crazy."

"Yes, I hope so."

The awkward silence closed in on him. Ava glanced toward the door. He couldn't let her leave without telling her how he felt.

"Ava, do you need some help with the girls?"

Was that really what he was asking, if she needed help? As if she'd let him live with them, marry her and be a father because it was good for the girls.

"What?" She looked confused.

Kee wiped his forehead. Knowing he was going to have to say it and take the risk. He was going to have to lay his heart out. He knew her and knew he could trust her. She wasn't interested in his position or any possible status that wedding a doctor would bring. She knew enough to know that his salary, whatever it would be, might be less than what she would've earned had she not lost her position.

"I wanted to ask you something, Ava. But I don't want it to sound as if you'd take it because you have to. You don't. I know that."

"Ask me what, Kee?"

"You don't have a job right now. So if you need help."

She lifted her hand before his face in the universal sign for stop.

"Are you offering me money?" She lifted her hand and then dropped it limply to her side as she stared up at the ceiling tiles and the fluorescent lights. "Oh, man. I completely misread you, us… I don't know." She met his gaze. All the hope drained out as her dark eyes hardened into something cold as frozen ground. "I have a job. I'm your new dispatcher. And I can raise those girls without your money."

Kee tucked his elbows in tight and rubbed the back of his neck.

"Ava, I wasn't offering money."

She flapped her arms. "What, then? You selling your truck?"

"I want to marry you."

Her pretty mouth dropped open and she gasped. Then it snapped shut and she scowled. Something in his chest blazed to life and then turned to ash. Was that his heart?

Ava met his gaze and he thought he saw something like sorrow in her eyes. The seconds dragged by with the centuries as he waited for her answer.

"I do not need you, Kee," she said.

And there it was. The rejection he had feared. How could he convince her that her self-reliance could exist inside a relationship? How could he convince her to love him?

Kee had made many rational arguments in his lifetime but there was just no way to make Ava love him with words.

"But," she said, "I also know that my life would be so much richer, not richer, *sweeter* with you by my side. I do not need you. But I want you. I want to share your days and nights and love you. And I want you to love me even when we both know I am less than perfect."

"Perfect is boring. Is that a yes?"

She slipped her arms around him. "That is an unqualified yes."

Sweet relief washed over him and he lifted his

head to emit a hoot of pure joy. The laughter that bubbled from his throat had a painful quality and he realized there were tears in his eyes.

"Oh, Kee." She pressed her forehead to his.

He wrapped her up in his arms and kissed her. When he finally let her slide to the floor and drew back they were both panting and the glimmer in her eyes had changed from joyful to needy.

The desire ricocheted through him as the shock splashed against mental images that he wanted to see with his own two eyes.

"All right, then. If either of us needs CPR afterward, we're in the right spot."

"Want to go back to my place?" she asked.

He glanced at his watch. Clinic didn't officially open for ninety minutes and Ava's sister's place was right down the road. He lifted his brows as all the weariness and the anxiety drained away, leaving nothing but anticipation.

"I'm still on call," he said.

"Oh, you're on call for me from this moment on, buster." Her wicked smile curled upward and the mischief glittering in her eyes promised that this woman would never bore and never cling.

"That's Dr. Buster, to you."

She laughed. "Whatever."

Ava wanted him for all the right reasons and her independence just made her willingness to be his wife all the sweeter.

"Right this way," she said, looping one finger with his and leading him out the door to her awaiting car. He followed and knew he would follow Ava anywhere.

* * * * *

Get 4 FREE REWARDS!

We'll send you 2 FREE Books plus 2 FREE Mystery Gifts.

Harlequin® Romantic Suspense books feature heart-racing sensuality and the promise of a sweeping romance set against the backdrop of suspense.

FREE
Value Over
$20

Get 4 FREE REWARDS!

We'll send you 2 FREE Books plus 2 FREE Mystery Gifts.

Harlequin Presents® books feature a sensational and sophisticated world of international romance where sinfully tempting heroes ignite passion.

FREE Value Over $20

YES! Please send me 2 FREE Harlequin Presents® novels and my 2 FREE gifts (gifts are worth about $10 retail). After receiving them, if I don't wish to receive any more books, I can return the shipping statement marked "cancel." If I don't cancel, I will receive 6 brand-new novels every month and be billed just $4.55 each for the regular-print edition or $5.55 each for the larger-print edition in the U.S., or $5.49 each for the regular-print edition or $5.99 each for the larger-print edition in Canada. That's a savings of at least 11% off the cover price! It's quite a bargain! Shipping and handling is just 50¢ per book in the U.S. and 75¢ per book in Canada*. I understand that accepting the 2 free books and gifts places me under no obligation to buy anything. I can always return a shipment and cancel at any time. The free books and gifts are mine to keep no matter what I decide.

Choose one: ☐ **Harlequin Presents®**
Regular-Print
(106/306 HDN GMYX)

☐ **Harlequin Presents®**
Larger-Print
(176/376 HDN GMYX)

Name (please print)

Address   Apt. #

City   State/Province   Zip/Postal Code

Mail to the **Reader Service:**
IN U.S.A.: P.O. Box 1341, Buffalo, NY 14240-8531
IN CANADA: P.O. Box 603, Fort Erie, Ontario L2A 5X3

Want to try two free books from another series? Call 1-800-873-8635 or visit www.ReaderService.com.
